"You seem to be the kind who wouldn't welcome ideas or initiative," Holly said. "Especially from girls," she added almost under her breath.

"Oh, girls are all right, they have their place," Steve responded. "Especially if they're pretty, like you. Or," he added quickly, "do you consider that an insult too?"

"Oh, come on." She gave him an amused look. "Okay, I'm willing to have a truce, just don't push me too far. Perhaps the best way will be to avoid each other as much as possible." She looked to him for agreement.

"Maybe." Their eyes met. "I'm not sure that's what I had in mind," Steve said. Then he busied himself with starting up the car and they spoke very little on the way home.

Other VAGABOND BOOKS you will also enjoy

A Time to Love, A Time to Mourn
  by Page Dixon
Blackbriar
  by William Sleator
Dear Lovey Hart, I Am Desperate
  by Ellen Conford
Gimme an H, Gimme an E, Gimme an L, Gimme a P
  by Frank Bonham
Kidnapping Mr. Tubbs
  by Don Schellie
Sometimes I Don't Love My Mother
  by Hila Colman

Girl Meets Boy

A novel by
Hila Colman

Vagabond Books

SCHOLASTIC BOOK SERVICES
New York Toronto London Auckland Sydney Tokyo

For Sesyle and Joan,
right there when you need them.

ISBN 0-590-31988-4

Copyright © 1982 by Hila Colman. All rights reserved. Published by Scholastic Book Services, a division of Scholastic Inc.

12 11 10 9 8 7 6 5 4 3 2 1   1   2 3 4 5 6 7/8

Printed in the U.S.A.   06

1

The minute she walked into the house Holly felt a sense of gloom. She couldn't put a finger on it; nothing was different. The usual junk mail was piled on the hall table, her mother's early spring flowers provided a splash of color against the dark walls, the broken umbrella stand was leaning lopsided as usual in the corner. Yet she had a distinct feeling of apprehension, like walking into a doctor's waiting room.

Then she smelled the cigar smoke drifting from the kitchen. Of course. Dad was home when he shouldn't be, at four o'clock in the afternoon. Holly wished she hadn't come home so early; she should have gone over to her friend Susan's house. Too late now. She was here and he was here, sitting in the kitchen smoking his inevitable cigar, reading every newspaper he could lay his hands on. As if somewhere in some news story he could find an answer to the reason why, almost overnight, his business had collapsed: no one was coming into his beautiful showroom to buy a new car. Or even a used one. As he said himself, he didn't have to read the papers to find out. He knew the reasons. Holly could rattle them off as well as he: inflation, recession, cars too big, gas too expensive . . . yet he kept on reading, looking for answers.

Holly stood at the kitchen door a minute and watched him. Just in the past few months he had aged; not that his hair had turned white, nor had he acquired a lot of new wrinkles. The difference was in the way he sat hunched up, and the bewildered, anxious expression on his face. John Swanson had been a buoyant, lively man, with a humorous smile and a ready wit. Now he always seemed preoccupied and remote, and Holly didn't know how to reach him. She loved him so much; the frustration sometimes turned her sympathy into anger. How dare he be so aloof in his pain and shut her out? Didn't he know she wanted to be close to him, that there were still things they could laugh about together to escape from the oppressive gloom?

"Hi, Dad." Holly dumped her books on the kitchen table.

"Hello, honey." He smiled when he looked at her. Lately that seemed to be the only time he did smile.

"You're home early." She shouldn't have said that. The minute the words were out she could see the cloud creep over his face.

"Yeah. No sense hanging around that morgue."

She gave him a sympathetic smile. But she

2

couldn't help thinking that maybe if he *had* stayed on, someone *might* have come in. Maybe someone coming home from work, maybe someone getting married, maybe, maybe . . . But he had given up. And, Holly reflected, the worst part was that her mother was not prodding him out of it.

She picked up an apple from a bowl on the kitchen table and bit into it. Holly felt frightened and confused: not only by the change in her father, but in her mother, too. They were both behaving in an opposite way from what she had learned to expect.

Holly loved her parents. As an only child she had gone everywhere with them. Even when she was a few weeks old, her mother had told her, they had taken her to parties in her little carrier. "You'd sleep right through like an angel," her mother said. Unlike many of her friends, Holly felt good about her family. "We have a good time together," she often said.

"Past tense," she thought now, wistfully. "We *had* a good time together." The trouble had started in the fall when her father had said he'd had the worst September since he'd been in business. And things had gone steadily downhill. Now, in the spring, when the automobile business usually picked up, it was at its worst. Her father came home from work earlier and earlier, more edgy, more morose.

"It isn't as if we were starving," Holly had said to her mother a few nights before. Mr. Swanson had gone out for a walk and they were doing the dinner dishes. "You have your job. You make pretty good money, don't you?"

"Enough." Her mother was frowning. She was a handsome woman, with the same strong face she had

3

given her daughter. They looked alike with their olive complexion and dark hair and finely cut features. "We have good bones," her mother was fond of saying. Now she glanced at Holly. "Sometimes I wish I wasn't working."

"Mom! I thought you believed women should be financially independent. That's what you're always telling me: 'Make your own money, don't be dependent on a man.' "

Lucy Swanson smiled. "I know. Maybe we can't always practice what we preach. My earning money now is hard on your dad."

"But we wouldn't have anything if you weren't working. That's silly." Holly stared at her mother unbelievingly. Her mother was a champion of women's rights and Holly admired her for it. She had worked hard campaigning for a woman mayor and was always trying to get promotions for the salesladies in the department store where she was a buyer.

"It hurts him, don't you see?" Mrs. Swanson scrubbed a pot fiercely. Then she turned to face Holly. "He can't stand having me earn money when he isn't."

"That doesn't make sense," Holly said bluntly. "What's the good of all the things you've said about women being equal and independent? If you lost your job, would he want to quit his?"

"No, but you can't always live by rules, don't you see? Not even the ones you make for yourself." Her mother, usually so confident, now seemed to be asking for her approval. "Right now he needs all the tender, loving care he can get."

"Well, yes," Holly said dubiously. "But that

doesn't mean you have to *wait* on him, does it? I mean, he's not sick. If he wants a cup of tea he can make it, can't he? He doesn't have to wait until you come home from work to make it for him. I don't think a woman should be a slave to a man. You never thought so either."

"I'm not being a slave," her mother said indignantly. Then she laughed ruefully. "Men are spoiled. They're used to being waited on and maybe we only have ourselves to blame."

Now, this rainy April afternoon was a repetition of all the days before. Mrs. Swanson worked hard in her job as a buyer for a chain of women's specialty shops in New England (the main store was in Boston and the Swansons lived in a suburb). No sooner had her mother come in and taken off her topcoat when she said, "John, darling, you want a cup of tea?" Holly gave her mother an amused glance and then looked away.

"While you're at it, make one for me, too, please," Holly said.

"You mean you haven't made tea all the time you've been home?" Mrs. Swanson spoke with a straight face, but her eyes were laughing at Holly.

"No, because you love to do it," Holly said with a grin.

"What are you two laughing about?" Mr. Swanson looked from one to the other.

"Female joke," Holly told him.

Holly took her cup of tea to her room and sat down at her desk. Her room was at the back of the house, and beyond the low houses on the street behind theirs she could see the hills of the surrounding countryside. Holly had once tried to figure out how many hours, in the twelve out of her sixteen years she'd lived in this house, she had spent looking out at her view. But after trying to figure out only one month's time of sitting, gazing, and daydreaming, she had given up. It was enough to say that she loved to sit there, and she was sure she did her best thinking looking out of that particular window.

While she sipped her tea her thoughts moved from her parents to herself, to school, and back to her parents. She felt oddly let down by her mother. She thought that if you believed in something you should live it, that you should practice what you preach. After all, Mrs. Swanson had been the one who had led the PTA in a battle for shop classes for girls. She was the one who had tried, less successfully, to convince the junior class that it was sexist to elect a beauty queen for the Junior Prom. But now, when there was a crisis at home, Holly felt she was abandoning her principles. Suddenly her mother was a woman scared to say boo to her husband.

When Holly got on the phone with her friend Susan, as she did almost every afternoon, she gave vent to her feelings. "I don't understand her," she said. "She waits on him hand and foot and he just accepts it like that's the way it's supposed to be. What's the good of all the things she's always said and done, if now she turns into one of those dopey women who act like the man is king?"

Susan laughed. "Maybe she likes to do it."

"That's what she says. Not me. I'm never going to get married anyway. I'd *never* wait on a man and

6

that's what they all want. That's what my mother *used* to say, that they all want to marry housekeepers. That leaves me out."

"Except when you fall in love," Susan said. "Then you'll change your mind."

"Not on your life. Never."

After Holly hung up the phone and brooded some more she took out the letter. Reading it every day had become a ritual, a reassurance of her worth and ability. For all her outward show of confidence, as Holly herself put it, there was a "pretty nervous kid underneath." She gazed at the letter lovingly: *We are happy to inform you that you have been chosen as one of our two junior counselors for the upcoming summer season at Camp Lillinonah. We look forward to seeing you at our get-together before camp opens on Tuesday, June 27th, on Lake Newfound, Hebron, New Hampshire. Details on transportation will be sent to you soon. Welcome to our family of counselors and campers.*

There it was, and no mistaking. Only Holly knew how nervous she had been when she had gone into Boston to the hotel for the interview: the big lobby, the well-dressed people, the noise, and the confusion.

When finally she had been ushered into the private suite of Mr. and Mrs. Miller, the camp owners, she had been in a cold sweat. They had asked a lot of questions and she had babbled on (her description) about how she had won her lifesaving emblem in swimming, reached the girls' finals in interschool tennis, played the flute, and loved nature, hiking, and small children more than anything in the world. The expressions on the faces of Mr. and Mrs. Miller had

7

remained impassive, and when Holly left she was positive she had made a fool of herself, that she would never hear from them again, and that she had better look for summer jobs mowing lawns or cleaning houses.

But that had not kept her from dashing for the mail every day with her heart thumping. When the letter had finally arrived she could hardly believe it, but her parents' reaction had been a letdown. They were too engrossed in their own trouble to share her excitement. After all, Holly thought, looking at the letter for the hundredth time, it's no big deal taking care of a bunch of kids for practically no pay. A free summer, yes, and she hoped some fun; but junior counselors, she had been told, got experience and very little money. Not even enough to buy her school clothes in the fall. But still she felt good about it. There had been a slew of applicants and she had been chosen. No one could take that away from her.

Yet her feeling of uneasiness lingered. She wished she had generated more excitement at home. This was her first real job even if the pay was peanuts.

"Okay, I'm coming." Holly answered her mother's call to dinner with little enthusiasm. Another dismal meal, with her mother's cheerfulness too depressing and her father's feeble attempt to show interest outside of his own trouble, sad.

At least the food was good. Holly did think her mother went overboard in "keeping things normal" by serving steak instead of hamburgers or chicken, yet she marveled at her mother's ability to work as hard as she did at her job and still put on an elegant meal at home. When Holly cooked she didn't fuss

8

with sauces or fine chopping or heating the bread and plates.

They were eating their salad when Mrs. Swanson said casually, "I was offered a new job today. A promotion."

"Terrific. What is it?" Holly asked excitedly.

"Yes, what is it?" her father repeated.

"They're opening a new suburban store in White Plains, New York. I've been asked to manage it. A lot of money, too."

"Oh, Mom. How super. That's marvelous."

Her mother was looking at her father, not at Holly. "I'm glad they finally appreciate you," Mr. Swanson said, pushing his plate back, leaving most of his food uneaten. "That's fine."

"I'm not taking it, of course." Mrs. Swanson busied herself cutting a slice of bread and buttering it.

"You're not!" Holly shrieked. "Why not?"

Mrs. Swanson glanced at her husband and back to her bread. "Lots of reasons. We don't want to move, do we? Dad has his business here, and you have your school. I'm happy to stay where I am."

Holly looked from one parent to the other. "Don't stay because of me," she mumbled.

"Nor me either," Mr. Swanson said. "It's probably a really good chance for you. My business isn't that important. Not now it isn't," he added bitterly.

"Of course it is. Jack, you know this is only temporary. You have a reputation here, a good one. You don't want to start all over again someplace else."

Mr. Swanson shrugged. "It's up to you."

Holly wanted to scream. He wasn't even urging

9

her to take it and she was giving it up just for him. It was hard to believe what was happening right in front of her eyes. Everything her mother preached and believed in going down the drain. How could her mother say no to a big, exciting job to stay stuck in something she'd been doing for ten years! And her father was right, his business wasn't that important anymore. Her mother was the one earning the money.

Holly asked to be excused and got up and left the table. She wasn't back in her room long before her mother came in. "You're disappointed in me, aren't you?" Mrs. Swanson asked softly. Holly was on her bed and her mother sat at the foot facing her.

"I don't understand you. I can't believe you'd give up an opportunity like this. Especially now, when Dad's not making any money. It doesn't make sense."

"I don't care about making sense." Mrs. Swanson's voice was tense. "It's precisely because he's not making money that I have to say no. Don't you see? It would be the end of him if I took this job and we had to move away. I don't think he'd ever recover, it would be such a blow to his ego."

"*His* ego? What about yours? You may never get a chance like this again. You're doing exactly what you've told me never to do. You've told me that a woman's career is as important as a man's. That if a woman is treated as second class it's partly because she lets herself be, that she lets the man be more important. Isn't that what you're doing right now?"

"I know." Her mother looked at her despondently.

10

"But there are times when one has to act by *feelings*, not principles. You'll understand when you're older. I love him and I don't want to hurt him. It's that simple. I hope someday you'll love someone, then you'll know."

"Not if it means sacrificing what I believe in. I'll never fall in love anyway. It spoils everything," Holly said, giving the footboard a kick with her foot. She looked at her mother's troubled face. "I love Dad, too. I love him very much."

"I know you do. Things will work out, you'll see." Mrs. Swanson didn't sound convincing, but she gave Holly a kiss and left. Holly opened a book but she couldn't concentrate, and she followed her mother back to the living room. "Want to play a game of Scrabble?" she asked her father.

"I don't think so, thanks." He was again surrounded by his newspapers.

"Maybe there's a good movie on TV, one of the old ones that you like."

Her father looked up from his paper. "Come over here."

Holly went to sit on the arm of his chair and he put his arm around her. "I'm not very good company these days, am I? No, I know it." He waved away her protest. "These are lousy times, but they won't last forever. Something's got to happen. I don't know what, but something. You're a good girl, honey, just be patient."

"Don't worry about me, I'm fine." Holly gave her father a hug and went back to her homework. But her mind kept wandering. For a whole year she had been waiting to be sixteen. "So now you are," she told herself, "and what's so great about it? Everything is more confused."

Big words she had said: I'm never going to fall in love. But why had she started thinking about it, all of a sudden? Why did she and Susan talk about the boys in their class, when they never used to? Why did she fuss about her tennis clothes now when she played with Michael, when she used to play in any old thing? Holly got up and looked at herself in the mirror: good hair, all-right face, flat stomach, proper curves, really good legs. She picked up her brush and brushed her hair furiously. At least if and when she ever did fall for someone it was going to be someone who didn't put her down because she was a female. If such a person existed. And, Holly added to herself, if I would ever be lucky enough to find him.

2

Of that spring Holly wrote in her journal: *It was too beautiful again today. I almost wished it would rain. I can't stand so much dazzling light and life when inside my house it seems dead. If I were the kind to fall in love, I would fall in love this spring. But there's only Michael to play tennis with and I could never fall for him. I've known him too long. I wonder if I'll meet someone this summer . . . Nuts. I'm not going to be one of those moony girls whose life depends upon a boyfriend. Period.*

"Your serve," Michael called. It was a soft Saturday morning in June. They had met early for their game before the sun got hot.

"Righto." Holly sent an ace across the net, the ball just hitting the serve line and bouncing off out of Michael's reach. "Fifteen-love."

"That was a beaut. Pretty good for a girl," Michael said with a grin. He enjoyed teasing Holly.

"You think so? Wait till you see this one." Holly poised herself for another kill, threw the ball up in the air, and smashed it hard with her racket. But this time the ball fell short and hit the net. "Damn."

Her second serve fared no better. "Fifteen-all." She lost the game on her own serve, losing the advantage she had had, and soon she lost the set to him 6–3. After two more sets, 7–5 and 6–4, both Holly's loss, they quit.

The midmorning sun was scorching when they walked off the courts. "I sure messed this up," Holly said disconsolately. "You never should have won the last set. To have you 4–4, and then to lose. My serving was really lousy."

Michael squinted his eyes against the sun and looked at her from under his bushy eyebrows. "You gave me a good game. Winning is important to you, isn't it?"

Holly gave him a swift glance. "Sure. It's part of the fun. Don't you play to win?"

"Sometimes. Sometimes I just like to play."

Holly stopped walking and faced him. "You tried to win today, didn't you?"

"I really didn't care that much." Michael ran his hand through his thick dark hair.

"You mean because you were playing with a girl? Come on, Mike, out with it."

"Darn it, Holly, it *is* different. I know everything you're going to say, I've heard it. A lot of it from you. Don't get me wrong, I didn't throw any points your way. But beating you wasn't that important, not

14

like when I play with Bill Diamond. We really go wild. This is more relaxing."

Holly stood with her nails digging into one closed fist, the other hand clenched around her racket. "You are a stinker. I can't believe you, one of my best friends. You really believe that playing a game with a girl is different from playing with a boy? Okay, Mike, I get the message. This is the last game of tennis I play with you," she said in a low, intense voice. "I'm not interested in giving you a rest hour on the tennis court." She turned to walk away, afraid that her angry tears would betray her.

Michael held her by the arm. "Come on, Holly. Don't be like that. You're too darn one-sided. I don't *want* everything with a girl to be the same as with a boy — that would be boring. Awful. It's just different, you gotta understand that. Don't make some big deal out of this. Please."

Holly shook her head impatiently. "I don't want to break up our friendship any more than you do. But it gets me mad to hear you say you give Bill a hard game, but with me it's relaxing. I mean, that's garbage. When you play you play, and my sex shouldn't make any difference."

Michael shrugged. "What can I say? You want me to be honest, so I'm honest. Your sex does make a difference and I can't say it doesn't. Come on, I'll buy you a Coke."

Holly gave him a rueful smile. "I lost — I'll buy *you* a Coke, big shot." Together they headed toward a nearby coffee shop.

* * *

After saying good-bye to Michael, she walked home slowly. Nothing had changed there. If anything, Holly felt the atmosphere had gotten worse. With the warm weather, when people used to buy cars, the slackness in her father's business became even more depressing. Her mother had not talked any further about the offer of the promotion, but Holly was sure her mother had some regrets. Once Holly found her sitting at her desk adding up a lot of figures, and her mother had torn up the paper when she saw Holly approach.

"What are you doing?" Holly had asked.

Her mother looked embarrassed. "I was figuring out what my take-home would have been if I'd taken that job. It makes me feel important to know I *could* have earned that much money."

"You should have taken the job," Holly said.

Her mother shook her head. "No, I did the right thing."

Holly didn't answer.

She was torn between being excited about going away for the summer to her first real job and pangs of guilt about leaving her parents at such a time. In two weeks she would join the group of counselors and staff going up to New Hampshire.

She was reluctant to go indoors. But she still had to sew name tapes on her clothes for camp.

"Hi, Mom." Her mother was in the kitchen ironing. "Where's Dad?"

"At work, of course. It's Saturday, usually a good day for him. Used to be," Mrs. Swanson added wistfully.

"Yeah, used to be." Holly put down her tennis

16

racket and peeled a banana for herself. She sat down at the kitchen table. "You think his business will ever pick up again?"

Her mother looked up to meet her eyes. "I certainly hope so." She gave a deep sigh.

"What'll happen if it doesn't?" Holly kept her eyes on her mother but Mrs. Swanson looked down at her ironing. She finished the shirt she was doing before she answered, "I don't know." She shook her head impatiently. "I'm not going to think about that. It will come back. It has to."

"You could go on working and Dad could stay home and take care of the house. You're doing more than you should anyway. Dad could learn to cook. I don't know why he doesn't do it now."

Mrs. Swanson put down the iron and looked at her daughter. "Of course he could learn. Anyone can learn to cook. But this would be the worst time in the world for your father to take up housekeeping and cooking. It would ruin him. He has to stick to the auto business, to go to work."

Holly stood up, dropped her banana peel into the garbage pail, and picked up her racket. She turned to her mother before leaving. "I don't get it. You're doing both and it's not ruining you. You talk big, being equal and all that, but you don't live it."

"I do believe in equality, you know that, but it's not that simple. Sometimes you have to retreat. Maybe things will be different for you, you're a new generation."

"You bet," Holly said. She went upstairs thoughtfully. That was it: for all her mother's forward-looking ideas about women, she couldn't possibly be totally free of all the old hang-ups. Her generation was stuck with them. I'm the lucky one, Holly thought; I'm going to be different. I'll never be a slavey to any man. No way. *If*, she said silently, adding the *if* that she always did, I should ever fall in love with anyone.

Holly went to her room to check off her clothes once more against the required list the camp had sent her: shorts, blouses, dungarees, heavy sweater, poncho, one long skirt, sleeping bag, canteen, flashlight, two blankets . . .

Holly thought about the long skirt. Did that mean dances? Parties? *Boys?* Holly sat with the list in her hand, looking out of her window. Maybe there would be someone . . . This spring she had felt longings stirring within herself, little twitches of jealousy when she had watched kids in her class become couples. For all her grandiose statements that she would never fall for anyone, she wondered more and more if there couldn't be a boy somewhere who felt as she did. A boy who believed that a girl was as smart as a boy, could be as strong as a boy. That even Michael, a very good friend, could be condescending to her had hurt; but, to her own surprise, her secret fantasies were not dashed. Even Susan, her best friend, did not know that big-talking Holly was watching, waiting for that special person to come along who would meet her on equal grounds, treat her as she wanted to be treated. Maybe she'd find a romance at Camp Lillinonah. Holly laughed at her own inconsistency.

* * *

It had not occurred to Holly to be nervous about leaving home. For several years she had gone on three- or four-day camping trips with the Audubon Society, but that had always been with a group of her own friends. Now, however, sitting in a van outside South Station in Boston with a dozen or so young people, not one of whom she knew, she suddenly felt anxious. With a sinking heart she watched her parents' car pull out of its parking space while she returned her mother's frantic waving as the car drove out of sight. It would be midsummer before she'd see them again, *if* they could manage to come up for parents' weekend.

In the meantime she was alone, on her own. That should make me feel good, she thought, and deliberately she reminded herself of all the times she had wanted to be left alone, not told what to do, dreaming of the time when she would be old enough to come and go as she pleased. The fluttering in her heart gradually quieted down, and she looked around the small bus to take stock of her fellow passengers. She didn't know whether they were all counselors or some were office and kitchen staff. There were clearly more young men than women.

The seat next to Holly's was empty and soon a tall, thin girl, with long, straight black hair almost down to her waist, came over to her. "Can I sit here?" She sat down without waiting for an answer although Holly quickly said, "Sure."

"I'm Melissa Claremont. Someone said you were the other junior counselor. There's just the two of us — you're the great outdoor one and I'm music and arts and crafts. I'm not outdoorsy at all, I'll die if I see a snake. Do you suppose there are snakes up there? I've never been to a camp in my life. I live in New York and Central Park is as far as I go in the country. I guess I'm insane to be here, but a job's a job. Tell me about you."

Holly felt as if she had to catch her breath. One look at the stiletto heels Melissa was wearing with her jeans and the brilliant scarlet polish on her nails had been enough to make Holly wonder why the girl was going to a camp. But her dark eyes were friendly and her sudden smile had an openness, even an innocence, that contradicted her surface sophistication. "What do you want to know?" Holly smiled, too.

"Everything. I'm wildly curious about people. My father says I should be a writer instead of a musician, but I haven't decided yet. What do you want to be?"

"I don't know. Maybe an anthropologist. I'm curious about people, too, but more about how different people live, and used to live. Or maybe I'll be a carpenter."

"A carpenter!" Melissa shrieked. "I never heard of a woman carpenter." She looked at Holly suspiciously. "You're one of those? Women's rights and all that stuff? You don't look it. You look all soft and feminine. You'll get over that, believe me. It's just a passing phase."

Holly laughed. "I doubt it. I really believe in it. But I'm not a fanatic, at least I don't think I am. I'm a simple country girl, honest." She said it with a grin, and Melissa laughed out loud.

"I'll bet you are. Like I'm a Nashville star. I think

20

I'm going to like you. You're one of the deep ones, I can tell. I'm psychic about people. Have you got a boyfriend?"

"I have friends who are boys but not what you would call a 'boyfriend.' What about you?"

"I always have a boyfriend. I fall in love easily. But it doesn't last. There are a few cute ones on this bus. I like the one standing up front near the driver's seat. The one with the curly blondish hair. He's neat. I'm terribly excited about this summer, aren't you?"

"Yeah. Nervous, too. This is my first real job." Holly thought the boy with the curly blondish hair was pretty neat, too. He was facing the bus, counting heads, and then speaking with the driver. She figured he was someone in charge. She liked the way he was built, graceful in his sweater and jeans, long legs and strong, too. Probably a terrific tennis player, she thought.

"He's staring at us," Melissa giggled. "My first job, too. Well, here we go." They were both thrown back in their seats as the van started with a jolt.

As the bus moved slowly through downtown Boston, the blond boy picked up a mike and addressed the group. "Welcome to Camp Lillinonah. I'm Steve Jackson, a senior counselor. I've got the title only because I've been going to Camp Lilly, as I fondly call it, since I've been around two." There was a scattering of laughter. "Thank you. Seriously, we don't think much of titles around camp. We've all got a job to do and we do it. Some of you are new and many of you have been here before, but we all work together gung-ho. But I'm not about to give

21

you a pep talk — I just want to say hello and welcome, don't be shy, introduce yourselves to each other. We're going to have a great summer." He grabbed hold of a handrail as the van came to a sudden stop for a changing light. "Provided, of course, we reach camp in one piece."

Holly turned around to talk to Melissa, but first she met Steve's eyes looking at her. She felt her face flush and was furious with herself. Melissa glanced at Steve and back to Holly. She laughed. "You're not wasting any time, are you? Just a simple country girl. Ha, ha."

3

It was late afternoon when the group arrived at camp. In the course of the ride, Holly learned that the older man with the beard was Joe Melotti, the camp cook; the rather prim-looking lady, Mrs. Olcott, was the nurse; the young men and a few women were assorted athletic counselors. She also learned that Steve Jackson came from Philadelphia and would be in charge of the waterfront, and that they would have two days of orientation before the campers arrived. The children would range in age from eight or nine to around twelve.

The van was met by Mr. and Mrs. Miller and a few staff members who were already there: the office secretary, the dietician, a couple of maintenance men, and kitchen helpers.

"It looks just like the picture on the brochure," Holly said, looking around.

Mrs. Miller heard her and laughed. "We didn't take a picture of some other place," she said.

The simple, weather-stained buildings were grouped around a more-or-less flat area called The Rectangle. The dormitory bunks were on one side, the social hall, dining hall, kitchen, library, and art room on the other. All sat on a low bluff facing the lake, where a freshly painted dock shone in the sun. Behind the buildings a hill led up to the ball fields, tennis courts, and several tents.

"It's beautiful," Holly said. She squeezed Melissa's arm. "Aren't you glad you came?"

"It's very pretty, but ask me a few weeks from now if I'm glad."

"I don't have to wait. I know I am."

"I hope you won't have to eat those words," Melissa said ominously.

Soon the truck with the luggage arrived, and after the confusion of everyone finding their own belongings, Holly and Melissa went in search of their bunks. "You're with the Midgets," Steve told Holly, and turning to Melissa, said that though she might have a couple of Midgets her girls would be mostly Intermediates. "The boys are up on the hill in the tents."

While theoretically Lillinonah was coed, the boys and girls were kept quite separate. They ate their meals together and used the same facilities, but their activities were organized differently and apart.

"How come the girls aren't in tents?" Holly asked. She picked up her suitcase to go down to the bunk Steve had indicated.

"They'd be miserable. They get hysterical if they

see a spider." Steve's face showed his disdain. He reached out to take the bag from her. "I can carry that for you."

"I can carry my own bag," Holly said coolly. "And I'm *not* afraid of spiders. Nor do I believe most little girls are."

"Oh, boy," Steve murmured. "One of those. Well, around here we still carry girls' luggage." He took the suitcase from her.

They stood facing each other. The sun made Steve's light hair shine, and Holly could see glints of red in the blondness. His eyes were as blue as the sky. Holly gave an impatient shake to her head. She had a fleeting vision of two people facing each other in a duel, each armed with a sword that could kill. Steve turned and strode ahead of her with the bag.

Holly followed, furious. It was nice of him to carry her bag and yet she had no doubt he wasn't just being nice. He was putting her in her place. Oh, boy! She wasn't going to let him spoil her summer, even if he was good-looking. Holly watched Melissa wheel her luggage in a cart down to her bunk and kicked herself for not having taken a cart herself.

"Here." Steve dumped her bag on the bed nearest the door. "This is your bed."

Holly looked at the six other beds in a neat row, three on each side of the long, narrow room. "Why is that one mine?"

Steve shrugged. "It just is. Always has been the counselor's."

"Well, maybe I'll decide to sleep in a different one. Or is there a rule against that?"

25

Steve's face was expressionless. "We do things a certain way around here and we like to do them that way. We're not big on change." His voice was amiable.

Holly met his eyes and she suppressed a smile. "Yes, sirree. Got it."

Steve's eyes blazed for a second, but then his face broke into a smile. "Glad you understand." He gave her a curt nod, and left. Holly stuck out her tongue at his receding back.

The next couple of days Holly was too busy to give much thought to Steve Jackson. The Millers were great believers in organization — they didn't like to leave much to chance — and consequently there were many meetings to set up programs and arrange who was to do what and when. Holly's schedule was changed several times, but finally she was set with a program that she could tack up on the wall next to her bed.

During those first few days the counselors fell into small groups of friends that would more or less carry them through the summer. Holly found herself part of a fivesome that included Melissa; Wendy Hill, the senior tennis counselor; Hal Balsam, a great soccer player; and Pee-Wee Cohen, who called himself "the man of all games."

The night before the campers were to arrive, Hal managed to get the camp jeep and the five of them went into town. "If you can call it a town," Pee-Wee commented, as they walked down the main street, with its one block of nondescript stores, a tiny old movie house playing two horror films no one had even heard of, a pizza parlor, and the firehouse.

When they tired of walking up and down the street they went into the pizza place. After they ordered, Hal looked at Melissa and Holly, the two newcomers, and asked them how they liked Lillinonah. He was a tall, slim boy who looked more studious than athletic.

"I like it, it's great," Melissa said.

"Yeah, it's okay," Holly agreed.

"You don't sound very enthusiastic," Wendy said to Holly. She was a blond, muscular girl — well built, although on the heavy side. She had an exuberant laugh that made everyone else laugh when she did.

"No, I do like it. Except for that Jackson guy. What's with him, anyway?"

"Steve?" Pee-Wee looked at Holly questioningly. Although shorter than average, Pee-Wee was considered the best-looking boy in camp. He had a strong face with even features, and amazingly bright, dark eyes rimmed with dramatically long lashes. "Our hardworking head counselor? He's okay. What have you got against him?"

"She thinks he's a chauvinist pig," Melissa said.

"I didn't say that," Holly cut in. "Although I wouldn't be surprised. He certainly puts girls down."

Wendy laughed her outrageous laughter. "Of course he does. But you shouldn't let it bother you. All men are chauvinists. Steve's no different."

"He's worse," Holly said. "And it does bother me. I hope I can avoid him this summer."

"You can't. Speak of the devil," Hal said, looking up at Steve coming to their table. "Did you hear us talking about you?"

27

"Something good I hope." Steve sat down next to Hal, directly opposite Holly. "Hope you don't mind my joining you."

"Most of us don't," Pee-Wee said.

Steve grinned. "I suspect I know someone who does mind," he said, looking straight at Holly.

She blushed. "The pizzas here are good, aren't they?" she said airily. Everyone laughed.

After that they chatted about camp, but Holly mainly listened. When they were ready to leave, Holly told Melissa she was going to the ladies' room and would meet them outside. But when she came out, only Steve was waiting at the door. "Where's everybody?" Holly looked around for the jeep but saw only the old, yellow VW that Steve had been driving.

"They left," Steve said.

Holly shook her head. "They wouldn't leave without me."

"They wouldn't but they did." Steve's face was inscrutable.

"What kind of a joke is this?" Holly started to walk away from him.

"You won't find them, they've gone. I told them I'd bring you home." Steve took her arm to guide her to the Volkswagen.

Holly swung free of him and faced him. "Don't you think that's rather a lot of nerve?" She was boiling.

"Maybe. Why don't you just calm down? I thought we ought to have a talk, and this seemed as good a time as any. Tomorrow the kids arrive and things will be hectic. I'm not going to bite you."

28

"I didn't think you would. But I do not like people butting into my affairs."

"Sorry. I apologize. However, you'll have to ride home with me. May I open the door for you, or is that against your principles, too?"

"Don't be a jackass," Holly said. Steve opened the car door and she got in.

They rode in silence until they were out of town. Steve drove slowly on the narrow country road that led to camp. When the blacktop turned into a dirt road through the woods, he pulled the car into a little clearing and stopped. Holly's eyes were wide and wary.

"Don't worry, I'm not going to molest you," Steve said with a grin. "It's easier talking this way than driving. I just thought we should come to an understanding. We seem to have got off on the wrong foot, but we're going to have to work together this summer, and I don't want to look forward to a summer of hassling. Do you?"

"No, of course not. I'm all for peace. But I suspect that getting along with you means doing everything your way, making all the concessions. I had thought that perhaps one reason I got the job was that the Millers thought I might have something to contribute. I wasn't just supposed to be a robot."

"It would take more than me to make a robot out of you. But whether you like it or not, I do happen to be in charge. Call me the boss if you like, although I don't like the word."

Holly moved uncomfortably in her seat. The woods on both sides of them were pitch-black, but the moon was coming up and the thought flashed

29

across Holly's mind that they were in a very romantic setting. Holly sighed. "There are bosses and bosses. You seem to be the kind who wouldn't welcome ideas or initiative. Especially from girls," she added, almost under her breath.

"Oh, girls are all right, they have their place," he said laughingly. "Especially if they're pretty, like you. Or," he added quickly, "do you consider that an insult, too?"

"Oh, come on." She gave him an amused look. "Okay, I'm willing to have a truce, just don't push me too far. Perhaps the best way will be to avoid each other as much as possible." She looked to him for agreement.

"Maybe." Their eyes met. "I'm not sure that's what I had in mind," Steve said. Then he busied himself with starting up the car, and they spoke very little on the way home.

Steve parked the car in an area behind the tennis courts, rather a long way from Holly's bunk. "I don't suppose you want me to walk you down there," Steve said. "Have you got a flashlight?"

"No, I didn't bring it." The path was very dark but Holly was not going to ask for help.

"Here, take mine. My tent's near here, and anyway I know every rock in this place."

"Thanks." Holly took his flashlight and walked carefully down the path. Before she went into her bunk she looked up at the moon breaking through the clouds and let out a deep sigh. What a pity, she thought, that an attractive, bright boy like Steve was so hung up on his darn male superiority.

That night Holly wrote in her journal: *I made a*

truce with Steve but I wonder if it will work. He is so all-out, big-shot male. It infuriates me. But sometimes when he looks at me I feel all shaky inside and that gets me madder than ever. Life is very complicated. I had the weirdest feeling tonight sitting in the car with Steve. I kept wondering what kind of a girl he really likes, and then thinking that I would hate her. But why should I care who he likes?

4

Holly knew, before her six young charges were barely unpacked, that Penny Stuart was going to be the problem child. "Every bunk has one," Wendy had warned her, "don't let it get you down. By the end of the summer she'll be a rah-rah camper."

Holly doubted that Penny would ever be rah-rah anything. She was a small, skinny girl with big, frightened eyes. She followed Holly around, clung to her as if losing sight of her would be the end of the world. The first afternoon, during rest hour after lunch, Penny complained of a stomachache.

"Do you want me to call the nurse?" Holly asked.

Penny looked more frightened. "No. If you sit here with me I think I'll feel better."

"I don't think my sitting with you can make your

omachache go away." But Holly sat down at the
ot of her bed.

"She's homesick," Sharon said. She was the oldest
rl of the group. "I was like that last year. It goes
way."

Holly stayed with Penny and talked with her, and
y the end of the rest hour, the child's face was
onsiderably brighter. Until Holly announced that it
as time for swimming. Five girls jumped up from
eir beds and put on their swimsuits, but Penny
urned her face into her pillow.

Holly motioned to the other girls to go outside
nd wait, and she sat down again beside Penny.
You don't like swimming, is that it?" she asked
ently.

A muffled sound came from the pillow. "Listen,
enny," Holly said. "You put on your bathing suit
nd come down to the water with me. I promise that
ou don't have to go into the water if you don't want
o. I can't leave you here alone, and the other girls
vant their swimming. Come on."

With some more persuasion, Penny put on her
vathing suit, and holding tight to Holly's hand, went
o the lake with her and the other girls. Holly and
ver five girls joined the other Midgets for their swimming lesson in the restricted area. Penny sat on the
hore and watched.

Holly could see Steve out on the raft with some of
he older campers. He was watching them dive off
he raft and swim to a buoy some twenty yards
way. She waved to him and then got busy with her
wn group. She lined up the children so that each

one in turn could show if she could swim and ho
well. When they were finished she divided them in
Beginners and Advanced, and then told them th
could all swim or play in the water for a few minut
until it was time to come out. There was a lot
splashing and fooling around, but everyone was ha
ing a good time, when Steve came over.

"Calm down, kids," Steve said. "This is a swim
ming lesson, not a free-for-all."

"I told them they could have some fun. They h
their lesson." Holly shook out her wet hair. She w
standing knee-deep in the water.

Steve gave her an appraising look that made h
aware of her clinging bathing suit and exposed bod
"We take swimming pretty seriously. I'll arrange
have Pee-Wee help you with the lessons."

"I can handle it. I simply thought they could pl
for a few minutes before coming out." She spok
very softly.

"I think you could use some help," he said, tryin
to duck a big splash coming his way. He blew h
whistle. "All out. One, two, three, everybody out

The children ran out and Holly followed slowl
Steve was standing next to Penny. "Why didn't sh
go in?"

"She didn't want to," Holly said calmly.

"Her parents want her to learn how to swim. T
get over her fear of the water. Remember," he sai
turning to Penny, "when you came with your moth
to see Mrs. Miller, you talked about it?"

Penny looked at Holly pleadingly. "Some oth
time I'll go in," she whispered.

"Some other time's now." Steve squatted so h

yes were level with Penny's. "Come in with me. I'll
hold you tight, and you don't have to put your head
in the water. Just walk in a little way with me. Come
on." He took her hand, but Penny started to whimper. "I can't go in. I have a stomachache —"

"I'll work with her on it," Holly said. "But I
wouldn't rush it."

"I've had kids like this before," Steve said, tugging Penny toward the water. "The longer you wait
the harder it is. Come on, Penny."

The child was crying now. "I don't want to go in.
Please don't make me."

"Leave her alone." Holly stooped down and put
her arms around Penny. She looked up at Steve, who
was glaring down at them. "I'll handle it."

Steve looked as if he wanted to say something,
shook his head angrily, then changed his mind again.
"You think you can handle everything, don't you?
Superwoman, aren't you?"

"No, just an ordinary female who doesn't like to
be pushed around." Holly stood up, holding firmly
on to Penny's hand. "And doesn't like to see anyone
else pushed around either."

"God deliver me from females like you. Thank
goodness they're not all like you."

"Unfortunately, they're not. Not yet, not until they
get wise. I suppose your girl, if you have one, just
adores to do everything you say."

"As a matter of fact, she does," Steve smiled complacently. "You could learn a thing or two from her.
When she comes up for a weekend, just watch."

"Oh boy. I can't wait." Still holding Penny by the
hand, Holly walked away toward their bunk. Penny

35

was skipping beside her, confident that she had a protector.

Holly was bursting with anger. She sent the girl off to take their showers and get dressed, and she went to look for Melissa. She had to unburden herself to someone. She found Melissa in the arts and crafts room, cleaning up after her last group. Holly picked up a broom and started to sweep the floor vigorously, welcoming the physical outlet for her frustration.

"What's the matter with you?" Melissa asked. "Either you killed someone or someone tried to kill you." Melissa spoke in her usual dramatic fashion.

"I wish I had killed someone." Holly put down the broom and put her hands on her hips. "I don't think I can hack that Steve Jackson for the rest of the summer. He's too much."

"What'd he do now?" Melissa asked mildly. She had been washing out paint brushes and now lined them up to dry.

Holly told her about the episode with Penny. "I can't stand his top sergeant tactics. This is a children's camp, not the army."

"Maybe he thought he was helping Penny," Melissa suggested timidly.

"He's not capable of thinking," Holly said scornfully. "With him it's he-man muscle, not brains. He told me his girlfriend was coming up for a weekend. I can just imagine what she's like, can't you?"

Melissa's smile often looked as if she had a secret, and she smiled that way now. "Do you care what she's like?"

"Of course not. I'm just curious."

36

Melissa laughed, but her eyes were very wise. "Curiosity is the perfect cover-up for a lot of things, jealousy, hate, even love. Sometimes all three."

Holly stared at her for a few seconds and then she gave a shrug and a light laugh. "I'm not that curious about anything to do with Steve Jackson."

"Of course not," Melissa said demurely, still with her enigmatic smile. "But I wonder why he even talked to you about his girlfriend. There'd be no reason why he'd want to make *you* jealous, is there?"

Holly laughed heartily this time. "Certainly not. Believe me, Steve and I come from different places. We're worlds apart. Let's forget about Steve."

Holly helped Melissa clean up the room, and the subject of Steve was dropped. But later Holly did wonder why Steve had made a point of telling her he had a girl and that she was very different from Holly. As if I would be interested, she thought, irked by the conversation, and then unreasonably annoyed because she was.

Camp was about two weeks into the season when, at a staff meeting, Hal said, "Isn't it time we had a staff party?"

Mr. and Mrs. Miller agreed it was a good idea, and Mrs. Miller told Steve to arrange it for the following Saturday night after the campers' lights-out.

After the business part of the meeting was over, Steve asked the counselors to stay and discuss the party. "Okay, Pee-Wee, you and I'll go into town to get the food. Hal, you take someone with you up to the woods for firewood, we're almost out. And the girls can take care of the set-up, coffee, and whatever has to be done to the food. Okay?"

Holly and Melissa exchanged glances.

"If we're going to fix the food, why don't we go in to town to get it?" Holly asked.

"Oh boy, here we go." Steve looked at her with an air of exaggerated resignation. "Because I don't think any of you can drive the jeep, that's why. It's a very peculiar and temperamental machine."

"That's quite an assumption. Naturally. Only a big he-man can drive it."

Pee-Wee laughed. "Naturally. How about we compromise, and Holly and I go in to get the food?"

"Or maybe Holly would like to go up and chop wood," Steve said.

"I probably could, although I've never handled a chain saw," Holly said calmly.

"Hurray. There's something the lady admits she can't do. What do you know? Can you believe it?" Steve laughed good-naturedly. "Tell you what, Holly and I will go in to get the food. How's that?" He turned to her.

She gave him a dangerous look. "It would be a pleasure," she said sweetly.

Holly left the meeting with Melissa. "What do you think he's up to?" she asked. "Why would he want me to go into town with him?"

"I think he likes you. No, honestly," she said to Holly's protest. "He likes to tease you, but he also likes you."

"Tease, my eye. He really believes men are superior to women, that's no fake. He gets me mad."

38

"The war between the sexes. You have a love-hate thing going."

"I don't *hate* him, but there's certainly no love."

"I'm not so sure," Melissa said with a sly grin.

"I'm sure." Holly let out an unexpected sigh. "This place is so beautiful," she said, looking around at the mountains and the sparkling blue of the lake. 'It would be a good place for some romance, *if* there was anyone around."

"The summer's just getting started, don't give up hope." Melissa sighed, too. "Maybe something will happen."

That night in her bunk, after the children were asleep, Holly sat at the window next to her bed, looking up at the sky. The stars seemed brighter here than at home, and she was sure there were more of them. She sat for a long time wrapped in a blanket looking out at the mountains outlined in the moonlight, enjoying the tangy pine-scented air. But her mood was not altogether a happy one.

She felt uneasy, restless, and disturbed. *I don't know where I'm at,* she had written in her journal. *Like I am on the brink of something but I don't know what. Sometimes the kids get on my nerves, and I wish I was home. Other times I love being here, but I keep expecting something big to happen. Yet every day the routine is the same, games, swimming, meals, etc. The summer seems as if it is going to last forever, yet it goes by so fast. I don't understand it.*

She didn't write in her journal how much she was

39

aware of Steve. It was as if putting into words all her vague feelings would make them too real, more real than she wanted to admit or to know. But not a day passed that she wasn't aware of his presence. She had felt him watching her down at the water, when finally she had gotten little Penny to at least walk into the lake. She had noticed him stop at the tennis courts when she had been giving her daily lesson. His eyes had followed her when she had gone into the kitchen that day at lunch to try to wangle some extra desserts for her table. She was conscious of him a dozen times a day, as if there were some invisible connection between them. The trouble was that she didn't know how to react. She didn't know if the connection was a good one or a bad one: if she should neatly and cleanly cut it, if she wanted to explore it further, or if she would do better to ignore it, pretend it didn't exist.

"The one thing I do know," she told herself in the dark, "is that it's driving me nuts. That boy Steve is the most attractive *and* pigheaded person I have ever known. I wish he had stayed home with that girl of his and that I had never met him." But Holly knew that that wasn't quite what she wanted either.

5

At breakfast on Friday, the day before the planned party, Steve came over to Holly and said that he had arranged for them to go into town that morning. Holly looked at him with surprise. "Who's taking over for me?"

"Your kids will skip tennis. They'll have arts and crafts with Melissa. Is that okay with you?" He looked as if he was expecting an argument.

"Sure. Except that —"

"Except that I should have discussed it with you first? Honestly, Holly . . ." He shook his head in despair.

"Okay, okay." Holly laughed good-naturedly. "It's your job to make these decisions, they're not important anyway, and you'll say I'm too sensitive. Okay?"

"Okay," Steve said. "I'll meet you in ten minutes up by the car."

Steve was in the jeep sitting behind the wheel when Holly arrived and climbed in beside him. Her concession to going into town was a clean white shirt tucked into her shorts, a sweater tied around her neck, and a pocketbook. They didn't talk much during the ride. Steve was concentrating on avoiding the holes and ruts in the dirt road, and Holly on holding on so that she wouldn't get thrown out of the open jeep.

They both sighed with relief when Steve parked the car on the main street. "Arriving without a breakdown is an accomplishment," Steve said. "I hope we're as lucky going home."

Buying the food for the party was a simple matter that didn't take more than twenty minutes. Holly wondered why it needed two of them to do it, and put the question to Steve. "Bureaucracy," he said concisely. "Also," he added, "it's more fun. Don't you think so?"

"Sure. Only . . ." She looked at him dubiously.

"Only what?"

"Only why did you pick me? Why not someone you like?"

Steve was holding their bags of groceries and he stooped to put them in the car before he answered. When he straightened himself up to his full, almost six-foot height he looked at her with a grin. "What makes you think I don't like you?"

Holly howled with laughter. "You don't exactly have a poker face. You disapprove of me completely.

You as much as told me you don't like independent women."

"I don't, as a group. How about we go and have a cup of coffee and talk about it?" Steve motioned to a coffee shop across the street.

"You aren't afraid camp will collapse if you don't get right back?" Holly looked up at him teasingly.

"That's mean, and I don't deserve it." Steve took her by the arm to steer her to the crossing.

"You're right. I take it back. I'm sorry."

"Okay. Come on, the light's green." Steve held her hand as they quickly crossed to the other side.

Steve got them coffee and doughnuts from the counter and they sat down in a corner booth opposite each other. "Okay. Now tell me where did you get all your ideas from? I suppose you read all those women's lib books?" Steve's voice was serious, free of sarcasm.

Holly believed he really wanted to know. She shook her head. "I haven't gotten them all from books. Sure, I read some of the stuff that's been written but mainly it's just what I see. A lot of the girls I know are smarter than the boys, or at least just as smart. I just can't see that men are superior in any way, and I think they've been assuming they're superior for too long. Women can run corporations, can run the government, can be lawyers, doctors; they can do any of those things as well as a man. So why shouldn't they?"

"There are a lot of reasons," Steve said. "Women are the ones who have babies. They're physiologically and psychologically different. I'm not saying women are stupid. Some of them I'm sure are

43

smarter than a lot of men. But they are different and they shouldn't compete with men."

Holly put down her coffee cup. "I don't believe you. That's such an old, tired cliché. You can't really mean it. My mother had a baby — she had me — and she's worked practically since I was born. As hard as my father, if not harder. Her physical differences didn't hamper her. I mean, what you're saying is hogwash."

Steve bristled. "Well, my mother didn't work. She stayed home and took care of my kid brother and me, and she did the cooking and cleaning, all the stuff that women do. She wouldn't take a job if you gave her a million dollars. And she's a pretty happy lady, let me tell you. I liked having her home — my brother and I were darn glad to have her there when we came home from school every day."

"I'll bet you were. Someone to give you milk and cookies. To wait on you hand and foot. And you'll want your wife to do the same." Holly turned up her nose in disgust.

"Darn right I will." Steve took a big bite of his doughnut.

"What if your wife wanted to go to work? What would you do?"

"My wife won't want to. You can count on that. The girl I'll marry will want to be a wife and a mother. Take care of me."

Holly laughed. "How come all you he-men need to be taken care of? Is that what your girl back home does? Take care of you?"

"You'd probably call her an old-fashioned girl. Maybe she is, but that's okay with me."

"Well, that's that." Holly pushed away her empty cup. "That takes care of that."

"Of what?" Steve picked up the check.

"Of any notion I had of working with you as an equal. You're the boss, I know it, you said as much, and I accept it." Holly closed her lips in a firm line.

"Oh, brother . . ." Steve stood up, scowling. He paid for their coffee and doughnuts, and Holly followed him out to the car.

When they had left the village and were on the camp road, Steve picked up the conversation. "I don't like titles, which is what I *did* say, and I don't like to be put on the defensive. I do happen to have certain responsibilities as a senior counselor, and you do happen to be new. But unless you are determined to make a monster of me I think we can work together very well."

Holly looked at him guilelessly. "Oh, Mr. Jackson, how can you say such a thing? Of course you're not a monster, you're a loveable, darling fellow." She paused for a few seconds before continuing. "Except for a small, retarded block in your otherwise fantastic brain."

Steve's face turned to her was grim, but when their eyes met, they both laughed. "I'm sure glad you appreciate my finer qualities," he murmured, and held her eyes until Holly turned away in confusion.

The staff party started off in the social hall. Melissa brought her guitar and sang songs, accompanied at the piano by Joe, the cook. Holly and Melissa had decided it would be fun to dress up, so they both wore their long skirts and put on eye makeup. When they came in together, Pee-Wee had let out a low wolf whistle and Steve said, "Wow."

"You look terrific," he said later to Holly.

"You look pretty good, too," she told him. She thought he looked super in fresh white ducks and a blue shirt. During the evening she could feel Steve's eyes on her, but it also dawned on her that Pee-Wee was staying very close. She liked Pee-Wee but she hoped he wasn't getting too interested in her. She didn't want to have to put him off.

After they had had enough of music and singing songs and talking, they went outside to the campfire that some of the boys had started. They roasted hot dogs, rolls, and marshmallows, and drank cold cider, and then sat around the fire and sang more songs. Holly found that Pee-Wee was sitting on one side of her and Melissa on the other. Getting cramped and feeling the chill of the night air, she put her arms around herself to warm up. Pee-Wee immediately took off the light jacket he wore over his sweater and put it around her shoulders. "Here, take his," he said.

"Oh, no, I'll be all right. You need it, thanks though."

Holly was about to give the jacket back to him, when Steve, who had been watching them from his side of the fire, spoke up. "Holly doesn't get cold. She's Superwoman. I thought everyone knew that."

"Maybe I don't know her as well as you do." Pee-Wee tied the sleeves of the jacket around Holly's shoulders.

"He doesn't know me at all," Holly said and gave Pee-Wee a grateful smile.

"Better than you think," Steve murmured.

"Enough to disapprove thoroughly. He doesn't like independent women," she explained to Pee-Wee.

Steve grunted something she didn't hear, but she was convinced it was something derogatory. Waves of hostility, she was sure, were flying across to her. "He really thinks men are superior," she said to Pee-Wee, loud enough for Steve to hear.

"Stuff it," Steve said.

"You mean you don't think so?" Holly knew she was pushing him too far, but it was too late to stop.

"I think this is a stupid conversation," he said coldly, got up, said good night to everyone, and left.

"I guess you got him mad," Melissa said with a giggle.

"I guess I did," Holly agreed. But she wasn't happy about it. Having Steve to spar with, she realized, was one of her more interesting occupations in camp. And yet it wasn't fun, she thought. It was more like having to touch a toothache, or run your fingers over a sore spot, as if a reminder of the hurt was a way of testing your feelings.

"He got me mad, too," Holly said. "He's got a talent for bringing out the worst in me." She stood up and the others were doing the same.

"I guess it's time to turn in," Hal said. He had been sitting next to Melissa.

"I'm not sleepy," Melissa said.

"Neither am I." Holly looked up at the dark sky and felt the nameless yearning that had been bothering her since spring, only tonight it was more acute, like a dull pain for which she could find no relief. "Let's do something," Holly said.

47

"What is there to do?" Melissa asked.

"I know what I'd like to do," Holly said after a minute or two watching the boys put out the fire. "I'd like to go out on the lake. Just glide silently in the night."

"Let's." Melissa's voice was excited. "That's a fantastic idea." She turned to Hal and Pee-Wee and asked them if they wanted to.

"Terrific," Pee-Wee agreed.

Hal was hesitant. "I don't think we're supposed to just take out a canoe. Steve'll get mad, he's in charge of the waterfront."

"He won't know," Pee-Wee said. "He's up in his tent sound asleep. We're counselors, not campers, and we're all good swimmers. Why shouldn't we go out in a canoe? Come on."

Hal didn't need much persuasion and soon the four of them were out on the lake in one of the large canoes. The girls had not bothered to change out of their long skirts, but they had all left their shoes on the dock. Pee-Wee was paddling stern and Holly bow, while Hal and Melissa were cuddled together in the middle of the boat.

Holly was glad that no one was talking. The swift motion of the canoe cutting silently through the water and the mysterious blackness of the night suited her mood perfectly. She felt elated, but in a quiet way, cut off from the petty problems of camp life: little Penny's anxieties, Sharon's pushiness, all the ups and downs of her young charges — and above all, Steve's provocativeness. This was peaceful but exciting, and what she had imagined camp life to be.

"Let's stop at the island," Pee-Wee said. Ahead of them was a small, thickly wooded island, whose shore was solid with rocks except for a small break where an inlet lapped against a tiny beach. Pee-Wee went directly for the beach. In a few minutes the girls were standing in the water, trying unsuccessfully to keep their skirts from getting wet while the boys pulled the boat up on the shore. The air was chilly but the water was warm. Holly thought that going swimming would be fantastic and was delighted when Pee-Wee suggested it. In seconds the boys were down to their briefs, and the girls dropped their skirts, took off their blouses, and in their underpants and bras ran into the water.

"This is heaven," Holly called out, swimming lazily, then turning on her back to float and look up at the sky. No one wanted to come out of the water because they knew they would be cold. Hal was the first to go out and they could see him shivering and rubbing himself dry with his shirt.

"We'll freeze," Melissa said to Holly.

"We can use our skirts. Mine's cotton so I don't care if I get it wet. I wash it anyway."

"Mine, too," Melissa agreed.

It was chilly out of the water, but Holly felt marvelous. "This was the best idea. I don't even mind my wet skirt," she said, putting it on after drying herself with it.

"It feels kind of icky, but I guess it'll be okay." Melissa tied on her wraparound. She laughed. "We were so afraid to get them wet when we first got out of the canoe."

The boys had been getting dressed on the other

side of the beach, and when Holly called out "All clear," they all went back to the canoe. Hal and Melissa offered to paddle back, but Holly, knowing that Melissa had never paddled in her life, said that she didn't mind, and Pee-Wee agreed.

The trip back to camp was swift, too short, Holly thought, and soon they were docking the canoe. They were being very quiet so as not to wake up the camp. They were just leaving the beached canoe and climbing over some rocks to get to the path when Melissa let out a piercing scream. "Oh my God," Pee-Wee groaned, and at the same time Holly and Hal grabbed hold of Melissa.

"What is it?" they said in unison.

"A snake, I saw a snake." She grabbed hold of Hal. "Get me out of here, please."

"Sh-sh, let's not make any noise," Hal warned, but it was too late. Mr. Miller was calling from the porch of his cabin, "Who's there? What's going on?"

"It's just us," Pee-Wee said softly. "A few of us were sitting down at the boathouse. One of the girls stepped on a stone, that's all."

"You kids better get to bed. You'll have the whole camp up if you make any more noise."

"Yes, sir." Pee-Wee turned to the others. "I guess that took care of him. Now let's be quiet."

Melissa was keeping a tight hold onto Hal as they went on up the path that led to the bunks and further on to the tents where the boys slept. Holly and Pee-Wee were walking in back of them and didn't see Steve coming down until he was in front of them. He had a sweater on over his pajamas and looked from one to the other. "What's going on?"

"Melissa thought she saw a snake," Hal told him.

"But what are you all doing here? It's late as hell." Then he noticed how wet they all were. "Were you swimming?"

"Yeah, over at the island," Pee-Wee told him.

Steve had his eyes on Holly. "You took out a boat?"

"Yes. What's wrong with that?" Holly asked, defensively.

"Plenty. You know darn well no one's supposed to take out a boat except with permission from me. I'm responsible for the waterfront." He spoke quietly but he was obviously angry.

"I thought we were both responsible," Holly's voice was equally quiet.

"You thought wrong."

They stood staring at each other while the others looked on. Finally Holly said in an easier tone, "This is pretty silly, isn't it, standing here at this hour of the night quibbling? So we took out a boat, we had a good time, and nothing happened. Don't be stuffy about it, Steve."

"I'm not being stuffy," he said vehemently. He glanced from her to Pee-Wee. "I'm glad you had a good time. Boys and girls *will* play," he added mockingly.

"Too bad you don't know how to," Holly said. "I'm going to bed. Good night." She turned and walked up the path to her bunk. A few minutes later there was a gentle knock on the door, and Melissa came in.

"He was jealous," Melissa said. "I think he would have liked to hit Pee-Wee."

51

"Don't be silly. He's not jealous of anyone, he's so full of himself." Holly was busy taking off her wet skirt. They were both whispering so as not to wake up the children.

"That may be, but I still think he was jealous. You two are something."

"We two are nothing," Holly said firmly. "We're worlds apart."

"Maybe." Melissa gave her a kiss and said good night.

In her bed, Holly thought about the evening with a sigh. Too bad Steve *was* so uptight. She wondered: If he brought out the worst in her, did she do the same to him? Probably with that silly girl of his at home he was adorable. Nuts. She wasn't going to stay awake all night thinking about Steve. It was a fun evening and she'd had a good time.

6

Sunday morning, Holly went up to the office to call her parents. While in all honesty she couldn't say that she thought about them all the time — she was much too busy and had her own problems — they were much on her mind, and she called them regularly. She knew that they both tried to sound cheerful when they spoke to her, but nothing had changed. Her father's business was no better, and her mother had given up her cleaning lady and was doing the house herself weekends. "Is Daddy helping you?" Holly asked.

"Yes, he's helping me." Her mother sounded irritated. "I suppose you've turned that camp upside-down by now? How are you getting on with that boy you said was giving you a hard time?"

"No better."

"Maybe you're giving him a hard time. Did you ever think of that?"

"I wish I were. Some woman should, he thinks men are so superior."

Her mother laughed. "I thought your generation was different. The boys, too."

"He's not. He belongs to the Dark Ages."

Holly was to use the same expression to Steve later that day.

They were at a staff meeting discussing an overnight hike the Midgets — both boys and girls — were going to take. As Steve outlined the plans, the girls would be out for one night and then get picked up in the truck to go back to camp. "The boys will go on for a second night and take the cog railway up Mt. Washington, sleep at the top overnight, and then come back."

"That's a much better trip," Holly objected. "Why can't the girls do the same?"

Steve gave her a weary look. "Because it's too much for them. It's a long trek just to get to the foot of Mt. Washington. It's a rough hike."

"I think some of the girls would like it. Can't those who want to go on do it? We have enough counselors to divide up the group. Let those that want to, go back, and the others stay out?" Holly looked around at the other counselors for support. Wendy spoke up.

"That's a good idea, why not?"

"I'm not so sure it's a good idea," Steve said. "I don't know if those kids are up to deciding if they can make it or not. You know those girls. 'I wanna do what my friend does.' " He said the last in a mock mincing voice.

Holly was ready to explode. "Steve, you are impossible. You honestly live in the Dark Ages. You really believe a girl can't think for herself as well as a boy can?"

"I think in that situation a girl is going to stick with her friends more than a boy would," Steve said decisively. "If a boy wants to play baseball he'll play it whether his best friend does or not. A girl clings to her group."

"I don't believe that for a minute," Holly said sharply. "And if it were true, it's because people like you won't give a girl a chance to come forward. You just rule it out." She was so angry she was close to tears, the last thing in the world she wanted.

"Let's decide about the trip," Pee-Wee said mildly. "Why don't we try Holly's suggestion this time and see how it works?"

"I'll discuss it with the Millers," Steve said curtly.

When Holly and Melissa left the meeting, Holly was still in a rage. "You take it all too seriously," Melissa said.

"I can't help it, that's the way I am. I really believe in equality for women, I think it's important. It's not just some trendy thing for me, I'm not trying to be stylish. I loathe discrimination — against any group." She gave Melissa a grin. "My great-grandmother was a suffragette. I guess it's in my blood."

"You certainly get Steve mad. But he *is* awfully cute. I love the way his hair curls, and his tan is

55

gorgeous. I could go for him but he doesn't even look at me — just you," she said.

"Oh, Melissa!" Holly was used to Melissa's chattering and she had learned not to pay attention.

To Holly's delight, the Millers agreed that if some of the girls wanted to hike and make the full trip, Holly could take them. They insisted, however, that one of the male counselors be with her in case she had any problems. "Sounds like Steve's fine hand," Holly commented to Melissa, "but I don't care. I'm excited, it should be a fantastic trip."

Four of the girls chose to take the longer trip: Sharon, her best friend Tammy, and two girls from Melissa's bunk, Tara and Lynn. Lynn was the youngest of the group, nine, and Sharon was the leader, a natural organizer. All four were pretty good athletes, and Holly felt she had a good, sturdy group. Pee-Wee volunteered to go with them, and he and Holly arranged for their provisions and divided up what had to be carried by the girls equally among their backpacks.

The first day was uneventful. Holly's little group stayed with the other girls. Because of a few stragglers they had to rest frequently and did not keep up with the boys ahead. When they arrived at the lake where they were to camp overnight, the boys already had a fire going to cook supper. Holly expected Steve, who had hiked with the boys, to make some remark about their being so slow, but he didn't. He simply distributed the tents and blankets that had arrived with the truck and suggested where to set them up. Holly and Pee-Wee decided to make their own fire for cooking, and soon they were all happily eating beans and hot dogs. It had been a long day and everyone went to bed early.

The next morning, the girls who were going back to camp were ready to take off in the truck by eight o'clock. Holly and Pee-Wee and the four girls who were going on stood waving good-bye. Steve came over and joined them. "Last chance," he called out. "Sure you don't want to go back?" he asked.

"We're sure," Sharon told him. "They're chicken."

"The boys are ready to go so we'll leave," Steve said to Holly. "You'll probably be slower anyway. We'll meet at the tip-top house. And don't forget, the last ride to the top leaves at four, so don't miss it."

"We'll be there," Holly assured him.

Their tents had gone back to camp on the truck, but it was close to half-past eight before they had their fire out, had cleaned up, and were ready to leave. Everyone was in a good mood — the girls especially pleased that they had chosen to go on with the trip. Sharon broke into a song and they all joined in as they followed the trail around the lake, and then onto an open dirt road.

"I should live in the woods," Holly said to Pee-Wee as they fell into stride on the road. "I love just wearing old clothes and camping out. I don't even miss TV. Maybe I should be a forest ranger."

"It would get lonesome," Pee-Wee said. "I like it, but only for so long. Then I want to go back to cars and fumes and noise and people, lots of people. I'm a city kid."

"That's the trouble. When I'm in the city I love that, too. I think how wonderful it is to see all kinds

57

of faces and buildings and smell different smells. There's so much to do," she said with a sigh. "I hope I get to do everything I want."

Pee-Wee gave her an admiring glance. "You will. You're stronger than most girls. I don't mean physically. I mean you know what you want and what you think."

"Lots of girls do. They just don't speak up. They've been brainwashed for too long."

Pee-Wee laughed. "Boy, you've got a one-track mind. Don't you ever think of anything else?"

Holly laughed sheepishly. "Yeah, I think of other things. The things girls are supposed to think of: clothes, my complexion, how I look . . . school, movies, TV. *Boys,* too, if you want to know. I'm not a freak. But once you start to notice how girls, women, are treated, it seems to pop up everywhere. It's weird."

She turned around to the girls who had slowed down. "Hey, come on, kids. Keep moving." She felt embarrassed by what Pee-Wee had said, and yet, she thought that if she hadn't spoken up, these girls wouldn't be having the good time that they were having. But she decided not to point that out to Pee-Wee.

Soon after the group stopped for lunch, they came to a small village with a country store. "Can we get ice cream?" Sharon asked. "I've got some money with me."

Holly looked to Pee-Wee. "I don't see why not, do you?"

Pee-Wee consulted his watch. "If they hurry up. We've still got a way to go and we don't want to miss

58

he last train." They all went into the store and got ice cream and the girls stopped to buy postcards. "To send our parents," they said.

"Come on, let's go." Pee-Wee was nervous. "We've got to get moving."

"We'll make it okay," Holly said reassuringly.

But Holly didn't know that the roughest part of the trail was still ahead. Narrow, winding paths, gorges to cross, steep hills to climb. In midafternoon, when the sun was hot, Lynn sat down. "Please, I've got to rest," she said. "My feet hurt. I've got blisters." She took off her sneakers and socks to show her red, sore feet.

"There's nothing we can do about them now," Holly told her. "I'll take care of them tonight. It isn't much farther, is it, Pee-Wee?"

He examined the map of the trail that he had. "It's hard to figure out. I don't know exactly where on the trail we are. It can't be very far. Come on, let's go."

Holly looked at the four girls anxiously. They were a pretty bedraggled crew. They all looked tired, and she wondered if she had done the right thing in pushing this trip. Lynn didn't want to put her sneakers back on, and Holly had to coax her. The kid looked as if she was in agony.

A good deal of the time they had been hiking they could see Mt. Washington in the distance, but now it kept looking as if they would reach it around the next bend. "Looks are deceiving," Pee-Wee said. "Almost there, but not quite."

Being that close, however, gave them a fresh spurt, and all six of them walked briskly. "There, there's

where the train leaves," Pee-Wee called out excitedly. "See —" Then he looked up and stopped in his
tracks. "Oh my God." His arm was outstretched and
his hand pointing. They could see a small railway car
starting up the side of the mountain. It looked like a
toy from where they were standing.

Holly stared in disbelief. "There must be another
one. That can't be the last."

"They wouldn't have two going up. I'm going to
find out." Pee-Wee, with a worried look on his face,
strode ahead. Holly and the girls followed.

Lynn was close to tears. "I can't walk so fast.
What'll we do if the train's gone? I need to ride."

Holly put her arm around the child to comfort
her. "We'll figure something out," she said.

Pee-Wee had raced ahead and they met him coming back from the station for the cog railway. Holly
knew from his face that the news was bad. "It's
left," he said simply. "We missed it by about five
minutes."

Lynn burst into tears and Holly put her arms
around her. "I'm glad," Sharon announced. "I didn't
want to ride anyway. Can we sleep out?" she asked
Holly.

"I don't know . . ." Holly was confused. She
didn't know what to do. She could hear Steve blam-
ing her, saying that he knew the girls couldn't make
the trip. She could just hear his voice saying, "Naturally you'd miss the train — those girls can't keep
up a steady pace."

Was it her fault? To miss the train by five minutes! The girls *had* been marvelous; they *had* kept up
a good pace — even poor little Lynn had been a

good sport. Holly did feel responsible, but she didn't think she had done anything wrong. She had been right, she told herself, to ask that the girls be given a chance for the trip, and their missing the train had nothing to do with it. It was just one of those things that happen. Her mind went back and forth distractedly.

Holly sat down in a clearing off the path. The others followed, with Lynn clinging close to her. Holly looked across at Pee-Wee who was nervously peeling a piece of bark. At a little after four, the sun was still quite high and hot, but the surrounding woods provided shade. Mt. Washington towered behind them. It felt good to sit down, Holly thought, and the serenity of the little glen they were in was reassuring. Holly began to feel excited by the situation: No real tragedy had occurred, and deciding what to do was a challenge. Together they would all figure something out.

She looked around at Pee-Wee and the girls. Lynn had her sneakers and socks off and was nursing her aching feet. Sharon was picking some wildflowers within reach of where she was sitting. Tammy and Tara were lying on their stomachs looking up at Holly with expectant faces. Pee-Wee was looking at her, too, his face still worried. Holly realized that they were all counting on her to solve their predicament. It gave her an odd feeling of both strength and awe. After all, Pee-Wee was a more experienced camper than she was, *and* a boy, but he, too, seemed to take for granted that she would know what to do.

"All right, kids, so we missed the train. I'm sorry,

but there's nothing we can do about it now." Holly's voice was matter-of-fact.

"It was Lynn's fault," Tammy said. "She was so slow."

"None of that," Holly said briskly. "Probably my fault if anyone's. But we're not looking to blame someone. Let's decide what we should do now."

"What can we do?" Lynn wailed.

"We can all go to a motel," Pee-Wee said jokingly.

"We could if we had the money." Holly became thoughtful. "The first thing to do, I think, is to get a message up to Steve. He won't know what happened to us."

She kept thinking of him saying, "I told you so."

"And how do you propose doing that?" Pee-Wee asked. "Send a note up with a pigeon?"

Holly laughed. "Wouldn't that be nice? Maybe we could turn you into a pigeon. No, but I imagine the railway can make some contact to the top. They could send up a message."

"Good thinking," Pee-Wee said admiringly. "I'll go find out." He was up in a second.

"Ask if there's a good campsite around here, too, please," Holly called after him.

"But we haven't any tents," Tara said, as they watched Pee-Wee take off.

"I know. Some of the trails have cabins for campers. If we don't find one, we'll sleep under the stars. It should be fun."

"If it doesn't rain," Lynn said gloomily.

Pee-Wee came back to report that a message would be sent to the railway at the top. They could still see the car chugging up the side of the mountain.

"But the fellow there said he didn't know about any cabins. He said the best thing is to stick to the trail and find a place we'd like to camp."

"I'd like a nice soft bed," Tammy said forlornly.

"Wouldn't we all," Holly agreed. But she was thinking more about food. She knew that the best way to cheer everyone up was to eat. But what? They had one can of beans left and a couple of hot dogs. Not enough for the six of them. Again she felt it was up to her. She had gotten them into this, she had to get them out.

"Didn't we pass a farmhouse back a way?" she asked no one in particular.

"Yes, there was a dog," Sharon said. "Mean-looking, too."

"I'm going back there to see if I can get us some food. Anyone want to come?" Holly stood up.

"Got any money?" Pee-Wee asked.

"About a dollar." She took some coins out of her pocket and counted them up: eighty-six cents.

"How do you expect to get enough food with that?"

"Ask for it. It's worth a try," Holly said.

The girls and Pee-Wee dug into their pockets and among them came up with a dollar and seventy-two cents. "Good," Holly said, "that makes a whole two dollars and fifty-eight cents. That should get us something."

"Not much. I'm starved," Pee-Wee said. "I'll go with you if you want."

"One of us should stay here." Holly looked to Sharon. "You want to come?"

Sharon agreed and they took off. The farmhouse

was about two miles back, but they retraced their steps quickly. The dog, a skinny animal, *was* mean-looking, and Holly was glad he was tied up. His owner, who appeared at a back door in response to the dog's vociferous barking, looked equally mean. She was a youngish woman with flaming red hair tied in a straggly knot, and a loud, angry voice. "We ain't got a telephone," she yelled at them.

"We don't want one," Holly called back, a little surprised.

"Campers always wanting to use a phone. What you want?"

"We'd like to get some food."

The woman looked at her with amazement. "We ain't a restaurant. What kind of food?"

Holly explained to her what had happened. She and Sharon were still standing at the gate, a good distance from the growling dog. "Got any money?" the woman asked.

"Not much. Two dollars and fifty-eight cents. What can you give us for that?"

"I dunno." The woman gave a harsh laugh. "I'll see." She vanished inside the house.

Holly went to open the gate and go up the path to the house, but Sharon held her back. "I don't want to go up there," Sharon said. "I'm scared."

"You wait here, I'll go." Holly walked up the dirt path to a back porch littered with an odd assort-ment: old motors, an ancient washing machine, a basket of fresh corn, a bowl of milk, and a broken doll carriage. Through the screen door she could see the kitchen, which, by comparison, looked clean and tidy.

"Here." The woman opened the door and thrust a large brown paper bag into her hand. "This should do you."

"That's marvelous. Thank you . . . I wish I had more money —"

"Give me a dollar, that's what I get for the eggs. Keep the rest." She gave a lopsided grin. "You may need it."

Holly was overwhelmed. "I don't know how to thank you —"

"Don't," the woman said abruptly. She saw Holly looking at the corn. "Pick out half a dozen, go ahead. I got work to do." She turned and went back into the house. She came to the door again and called to Holly. "You got a pan to cook with on your fire?"

Holly felt extraordinarily moved by the question. "Yeah, we got some camping stuff with us. Thanks a lot."

"You never know with city kids," the woman mumbled and disappeared again.

As soon as they were out of sight of the house, Holly stopped so they could examine what was in the bag. Besides the corn there were a dozen eggs, country bacon cut into thick slices, a loaf of fresh bread, and some apples. "What a feast!" On the walk back Holly kept thinking about the red-haired woman. She wondered if she lived way out in the woods there by herself, and wished she knew more about her. "She's a fantastic woman," she said aloud.

"At first I was scared of her," Sharon said.

"I like her. I bet she never heard of women's lib, but she's it, just naturally. No man could push her around. She was awfully generous, too. I'd like to be like that." Holly handed Sharon an apple and bit into one herself.

Sharon gave her a shy glance. "You are in a way. I don't mean you look like her," she added hastily. "I mean in saying what you think. Like asking for us to take this trip."

"I hope it turns out all right." Holly was wondering where they would spend the night.

As Holly had hoped, building a fire and cooking and eating cheered everyone up considerably. "I don't know why we don't just camp here," Pee-Wee suggested, after they had finished supper and were sitting around the fire. Fortunately, it was not a cold night, and the sky was brilliant with stars.

"Right out in the open?" Lynn asked nervously.

"Will there be any animals?" Tammy asked.

"No, I don't think so," Holly said with more assurance than she felt. "We'll keep the fire going, that'll keep them away."

The girls snuggled down together and were soon asleep. Holly and Pee-Wee napped more than really sleeping, taking turns to get up to throw another piece of wood on the fire. It was with great relief that Holly finally watched the sky brighten and the sun begin to come up behind the mountain.

7

When Holly, Pee-Wee, and the four girls, with Lynn limping, made it into camp late that day, the campers were in the dining hall having supper. Earlier Holly had been able to call camp to let them know what what happened and to tell them that they were all right. She didn't want to leave it to Steve to make the explanations when he and his group got back in the truck.

Mrs. Miller stood up to greet them, and then as one, the camp stood up and gave a cheer for the bedraggled hikers. First they cheered the group as a whole, and then they gave a cheer for Holly. Holly could feel her face go scarlet, and she was overwhelmed. She threw a glance over toward Steve, but he seemed to be studying a spot on the wall with a stoical face. He was standing up with the others but Holly didn't think he joined in the cheering.

After supper when most of the camp lolled around The Rectangle before going off to their various activities, Holly found herself near Steve. He came over to her. "You're a heroine," he said.

"You don't like them?" It was hard to know whether Steve was serious or mocking her.

"Oh, they have their place." He sat down on a rock beside her.

"Yeah, I know, conquering their pots and pans in the kitchen."

"Absolutely. Also mopping the floor and ironing their menfolks' shirts." He *was* mocking her.

"Said he earnestly. Does your girl embroider and play the harpsichord for you? Must make a pretty picture. Right out of Jane Austen. I suppose she calls you Mr. Jackson." Holly smiled at him pleasantly.

"Not a bad idea. Women should show respect for their lords and masters. Wouldn't be so many divorces and broken homes." He glanced at her sideways to see the effect of his words.

"You pretend to be joking but you really mean it." Holly stood up. "You are impossible. You are the most reactionary, pigheaded, chauvinist man I have ever heard of. I can't believe anyone can live in this world and be so blind. I can't talk to you, there's no use." She started to walk away, but Steve grabbed her by both her arms. They were facing each other on a large, flat rock that jutted out over the lake. For a second Holly thought that they might both topple over into the water. She stared unflinchingly into Steve's eyes.

"You can't talk to me that way." He had a tight

hold on her arms. "You're the one who's blind. Just because a man disagrees with you, all you can think of is to put him down. Women have done a lot of things in this world, but it hasn't been by imitating men. I'm not ashamed to believe that a woman should stay home and take care of her house and her kids. And I bet those women who did embroidery and played music were a darn sight happier than the discontented ones running around today."

"Like fun they were. They were miserable, neurotic women having fainting spells all the time. You don't know anything about it."

They stood glaring at each other. "You're hurting me," Holly said after a minute or two.

"I'm sorry." Steve let go of her arms.

Holly turned abruptly and walked away quickly. She ran back to her bunk to regain her composure. She sat on her bed and rubbed her arms where she could still feel the pressure of his hands. If she had been a boy she would have struck out and hit him — she could understand now why men got into fist fights. She would have liked to punch him and pummel him. The violence of her feelings, of her desire for a physical outlet, frightened her. Damn Steve Jackson, damn him.

For the next few days after that encounter Holly tried to ignore Steve. But it was impossible. They had to talk to each other at staff meetings, down at the waterfront, up at the tennis courts. Steve acted as if nothing had happened. That infuriated her as much as anything.

"He acts so superior," she said to Melissa one

night, after Steve had come over to them in the dining hall to tell them that the following Wednesday was their day off. "He thinks he can say all those things and I'm supposed to just accept them. 'Yes, m'lord, you're absolutely right —' Nuts. He picked on the wrong girl this time."

Melissa laughed. " 'Methinks the lady doth protest too much.' I think opposites attract, don't you? I mean, I usually fall for these terribly serious boys and you know how silly I am. And I'm dark and my boyfriends are always blond —"

Holly was only half-listening to Melissa's chatter. Her eyes were following Steve walking lazily across The Rectangle. He was wearing white shorts that emphasized his tanned skin, and the summer had slimmed him down and hardened his muscles. The late afternoon sun reflected in the lake below gave a rosy glow to all of them grouped around talking quietly. Suddenly Steve stopped and turned around and his eyes met Holly's. They held each other for a long minute. Melissa stopped talking and looked from one to the other until Holly pulled her eyes away. It was a strange moment — a sudden hushed moment, as if somehow, with their eyes locked, she and Steve had embraced.

Melissa looked at her curiously. "You do like him, I can tell."

"Don't be silly," Holly said, but her heart was racing.

"What are you going to do?" Melissa asked the following Wednesday morning. She was up at the infirmary with a swollen, sprained ankle, and Holly had come to visit her. The two girls had planned to take a day's trip together on their day off.

"I guess I'll just bum a ride into town. There's nothing much else to do."

"I'm sorry," Melissa said.

"It's not your fault."

Holly was disappointed. She had been looking forward to a day away from camp, and she and Melissa had discussed various places they could have gone.

Soon Holly said good-bye to Melissa and walked up the road leading out of camp. She had already had breakfast, attended to her morning chores, and kissed her young charges good-bye. Penny had clung to her, as if afraid she would be gone forever, but Holly had assured her that she would be back for supper that evening.

When she left the camp property and struck out on the wooded dirt road that led to the highway, Holly felt a sense of adventure. This was the first time she would be leaving camp by herself, and although she missed Melissa, it was exciting to have a whole day free to go exploring. In a way it was even a relief not to have Melissa's constant chatter. Just to feel the soft ground under her feet, to smell the pines, to hear the raucous call of a blue jay scolding its mate, not to have to think about anything — this was heaven. Holly walked along feeling herself a creature of the woods, with every sense quivering in response to her surroundings.

As she approached the highway she slowed her steps. She wasn't in a hurry to leave the woods. Once on the highway Holly knew the magic would be gone;

71

she would have to hitch a ride, go into town, decide what she wanted to do. For a moment she considered roaming the woods all day by herself, but then she remembered the stories she'd heard of people getting lost; and she had no compass, no camping equipment, so she decided against it. She was near enough to the highway to hear the cars when she sat down on a rock alongside the road to plan her day. There weren't many choices. Actually, she couldn't think of anything to do other than walk around the town, buy herself a pizza, probably look into some of the shops, and go back to camp. The trips that she and Melissa had discussed were not any that she cared to do alone.

She was still sitting there, just feeling lazy, when the camp jeep came down the road and stopped. Steve was driving it. "Hi," he said. "What are you doing?"

"Just sitting."

"Do you plan to spend your day off here?"

"I might. It's peaceful."

Steve laughed. "I never thought being peaceful was your bag."

"Just goes to show."

"Want a ride into town?"

Holly stood up. "I don't mind. That is, if you can stand it."

"I can stand it," he said tersely and leaned over to open the door for her.

They drove in silence for several minutes until Steve spoke. "What do you plan to do today?"

"Nothing much. There's nothing much to do, is there?"

72

"You want to go to Lost River?"

Holly turned around to look at him. "What do you mean?"

Steve kept his eyes on the road. "I mean do you want to go to Lost River? What do you think I mean? It's an interesting trip."

"You mean you and me?"

Steve turned to her. "For Pete's sake. Yes, Holly, I mean you and me. Holly and Steve. Is that impossible?"

Holly shook her head. "I suppose it's not impossible, but it certainly is peculiar. Is this your day off, too?"

"Yes. And if you're wondering if I planned it this way, I didn't. Pee-Wee asked me to switch with him and this is the way it turned out. But let's get this straight." He spoke hurriedly as if he wanted to get out what he had to say quickly. "It's your day off and mine. I have the car. I don't see why we couldn't do something together. I'm not trying to attach myself to you. I have a girl back home I'm crazy about, and I'm sure you have your own boyfriend. Besides, we have different ideas about things. But we could declare a moratorium and have a good time for a day, or even for the summer. I don't see anything wrong with that, do you?"

Holly kept looking at him in some astonishment. "A peace offering — just for the summer. Mmm, that's quite interesting."

"You don't sound very enthusiastic."

"I have to think about it. What would your girl think? That is, if we became friends?"

73

"She wouldn't mind. Why should she?" He gave Holly a sideways glance. "We *would* just be friends."

"You can bet on that. That is, if we *could* be friends."

"We can try."

"I suppose," Holly agreed hesitatingly. "Well. Tell me about Lost River. What is it and where is it?"

"It's about an hour-and-a-half's drive from here, a fantastic place. An underground river, you follow it through caves. Some places you have to crawl on your belly. Maybe it would be too rough for you?" Steve looked at her inquiringly.

"You've done it, haven't you?"

"Yes."

"Then I imagine I can." Holly gave him a swift glance and looked away. The thought flashed across Holly's mind that Steve could be up to something: Perhaps he was deliberately taking her to Lost River in the hope that she couldn't do it. She pushed the thought aside; it was too unpleasant.

"I think we should stop in town and buy a picnic lunch," Steve said.

They got themselves thick roast beef sandwiches, sodas, and chips, and when they got back into the jeep Holly made up her mind to enjoy herself. The morning haze had lifted and the day turned out to be sunny but not too warm, a perfect summer mountain day. If they avoided controversial subjects, Holly decided, she and Steve could get along. They were traveling through magnificent mountain country, and as they drove Holly's spirits rose. She began to sing. Unconsciously she picked a rather plaintive love song.

"That's nice," Steve said. "You sing that to your boyfriend?"

"I don't have *a* boyfriend. I have friends. Some are girls and some are boys."

"Then you've never been in love."

"No, I've never been in love." Holly felt they were on dangerous ground, so she pointed to a mountain range and asked the name of it. For the rest of the ride Steve pointed out the various spots of interest, and their conversation remained inconsequential.

When they arrived at Lost River, Steve parked the jeep and they found a pleasant grassy spot to have their lunch. Holly stretched out on her back, her head resting on her arms, and looked up at the sky, the brown bag of food unopened beside her.

She raised her head a bit so that she could see Steve, thinking how nice it was to be there and how pleasant Steve could be if only he weren't so macho. Right now when he was quiet and relaxed, not ordering her or anyone else around as he did at camp, it was easy to like him.

"I'm starved. Don't you want to eat?" Steve asked.

"Sure." Holly stretched herself but she didn't make any move to get the lunch. After a few minutes Steve opened the bag and took out their sandwiches. "Where are the paper napkins?"

"I don't know." Holly sat up. "Aren't there any?"

"No. Didn't you ask for them?"

"No. Did you?"

They stared at each other silently. "I assumed you would think of it," Steve said with a trace of annoyance.

Holly continued to hold his eyes and then she

burst out laughing. "I'm a failure. No doubt about it. Imagine the little woman forgetting paper napkins. Or daring to assume that maybe a great big he-man would think of a little itty-bitty thing like that."

"Oh, lay off," he said dangerously.

"Come on, Steve, laugh. It *is* funny. I mean, as things are between us, this is kind of our relationship in a nutshell, isn't it? We can call it the Paper Napkin War. Just for the summer . . ."

Steve gave her a sheepish grin. "Wars eventually come to an end, this one never will. I'm not going to change my mind and I don't suppose you will either. We can call it the Never-Ending Caper."

"It will end. Remember, just for the summer." Holly gave him a solemn look.

"Yeah," Steve said unconvincingly.

When they had finished eating, Steve led her to the caves. The entrance to the Lost River was a large cave that a tall person could stand up in. Ahead of them the water was flowing through a narrow passage and tumbling over rocks. They advanced slowly, single file, Steve in the lead. It took a few minutes for Holly's eyes to get accustomed to the semidarkness, but once they did, she kept discovering formations and colors of rocks that made her exclaim with delight.

"It's another world," she said to Steve. "To think that all this is underground. I wonder who discovered it was here? I expect to see leprechauns appear any minute."

"Mermaids would be more interesting," Steve remarked.

It was indeed a unique sight and experience. They stepped from rock to rock, often able to touch both sides of the cave wall with their hands, other times coming out into an idyllic, clear pool. The sound of the water never ceased as it spilled over the rocks, often showering them with its spray. Steve turned around frequently with an anxious "Are you all right?"

"Sure, I'm fine," Holly told him. The third or fourth time he asked, she said, "You don't have to worry about me. I'm okay."

"Yeah, I forget. Superwoman."

Holly let it go by. She was enjoying herself too much to have another argument.

"We're coming to the rough part now," Steve said, pointing ahead. It looked to Holly as if they were coming to the end, up against a solid wall of rock. But when she got closer she saw that there was a very narrow passage cut through it. "You have to really squeeze to get through this," Steve said. "A fat person can't do it. At the other side there's a pool and you have to pull yourself up onto a ledge above it. I'll go first and give you a hand."

"I'll manage," Holly said.

She followed Steve through the narrow passage, and then watched him step around the pool, and pull himself up to a smooth rock ledge about six feet above them. Impassively, he moved out of the way so that she could do the same. Holly was a good eight or nine inches shorter than Steve and her heart sank when she looked up at the ledge. But she was determined not to ask him for help, and, as she expected after her remark, he didn't offer. She wished he wasn't watching her though; his intense scrutiny made her uneasy.

Holly reached up and grabbed the edge of the ledge. But it was wet and slippery and her feet were barely off the ground before she lost her grasp. Steve's hand reached out, but Holly ignored it. She stepped on a rock near the pool's edge, to give herself more height and better leverage, and again grasped the ledge above her. This time she felt more secure. Willing all her strength into her hands she pulled herself up again. She was sure she was making it, with one knee almost on the rock above her, when she lost her grip and slid back down, this time into the pool of water up to her knees.

She looked up to see Steve trying hard to control his laughter. "I'm sorry," he spluttered. "But it was funny. The expression on your face . . . you looked so surprised . . . Honestly, I'm sorry."

Holly took herself out of the water onto a piece of dry ground. "I'm soaked." She looked up to Steve again and started to laugh herself. "Some superwoman . . . ugh, a real bummer." She sat down and took off her wet sneakers and socks, and handed them up to Steve. "Well, one more try."

"Still don't want any help? There are no prizes, you know."

"Yeah, I know." She gave him a grin. "It's my pride, man, my wet, soggy, barefoot pride. 'Anything you can do I can do . . .' " she sang gaily.

"Maybe," Steve said, also grinning.

"No maybe." This time Holly grabbed hold of the ledge and swung herself up with ease. She sat down next to Steve feeling very smug. "I don't know

78

why I didn't do it the first time. Should have taken my sneakers off."

"What are you going to do now with those wet things?" Steve indicated her sorry-looking sneakers and socks.

"Go barefoot."

"You can't on these rocks."

"Yes, I can. Why not?"

Steve studied her face. "Real tough, aren't you?"

Holly frowned. "I'm not tough, at least I hope not. I'm —" She caught him looking at her and she turned away. "I don't know what I am." She felt flustered.

Steve, too, suddenly seemed embarrassed. He stood up and said rather stiffly, "Let's get moving."

"Okay." Holly gathered up her wet things.

Going the rest of the way barefoot wasn't easy, but Holly managed without any more falls. However, she was glad to get out of the tunnel into the daylight again, and the soft grass felt good under her feet. She and Steve were strangely silent as they walked to the car.

"That was fun," Holly said when they were once again on the road.

"I had a good time," he said but his face was on the glum side. She wondered what he was thinking.

"It probably would have been better if you'd had your girl with you," Holly said.

"This isn't her kind of thing," he said curtly.

"What's she like? You haven't told me much about her, except she's very feminine."

"You'll meet her. I think she's coming up one weekend before camp's over."

79

"Terrific. I hope she does. That'll be great for you."

He didn't say anything and Holly was appalled by the way her own spirits drooped. She felt absolutely blah, and then told herself that was ridiculous: Why should I care if his silly girl is coming up? He doesn't mean a thing to me.

During the next few days, Holly's feeling of depression did not go away. A pall seemed to hang over everything she did, and Steve's words, *I have a girl back home I'm crazy about,* kept repeating in her head. She tried to convince herself that she was depressed because of her parents. Her telephone conversations with them certainly did not improve her mood, but she urged them to come up for parents' weekend. She was very eager to see them.

She especially hoped to have a chance to talk to her mother about her own mixed-up feelings. She had to finally admit to herself that her depression had to do with Steve. "But," as she said to Melissa, "it isn't only that I know he could never like someone like me, but that I should be interested in him is what gets me down. It's ridiculous. It makes me feel simple-minded, as if everything I believe in doesn't count for beans when some good-looking, macho boy comes along."

"Steve is more than that and you know it," Melissa said. "Besides, it's chemistry, love. Very few people fall in love because of ideas."

"I am not in love," Holly insisted.

Yet she felt that she was helplessly sliding into an emotional state she did not want. She would find herself in a situation less than admirable, and similar to one for which she had criticized her mother, a compromise of her own beliefs. It's crazy, she told herself. First of all he doesn't give a hoot for me, and even if he did, which he doesn't, his idea of a woman is the direct opposite of mine.

Holly felt that she could get through the rest of the summer okay if she didn't have to see Steve so much. But he was there and much as she tried, it was hard to avoid him. Worse than that, to her great discomfort and annoyance, he seemed more attractive than ever. It was almost as if he were going out of his way to impress upon her how nice he was.

It was a few days after their day together that he came over to her and her group at the lake. "Let's see how your kids are doing," he said jovially. He picked Penny up in his arms. "How about you? You like the water now?"

"Yes," she giggled, obviously pleased by his attention.

He put her down gently and told the children to go into the water. He put them through some paces of swimming under water, doing the dog paddle. Then he had each girl show him her best stroke.

When they were finished, he let them play, climb on his back and roll off, duck him, and splash around quite wildly.

Holly stood aside watching, until Steve dove for her and pulled her into the game. He went after her and pulled her under the water and then up into his arms. The physical contact with him was electrifying, but the thought flashed through Holly's head that his girl would very probably never let him see her with her face streaked with water and her hair streaming wet. Steve seemed as flustered as she at finding themselves so closely entwined, and they both pulled away abruptly. "Friends, just for the summer . . ." Holly thought silently.

But small things like that kept happening. In the dining hall that evening he picked up her sweater, which had fallen from the back of her chair, and put it around her shoulders. She hadn't even known it was him until she turned around and found him standing over her, smiling. When their eyes met, and she thanked him, he backed away quickly.

Two days later he turned up at the tennis courts when she was playing with Wendy. He simply sat and watched, but he made Holly nervous. She started serving double faults and swearing under her breath.

"Am I making you nervous?" Steve asked amiably after she'd made her third double fault.

"No, why should you?" Holly said crossly.

"I don't know. I shouldn't, but maybe I do."

"Don't flatter yourself. I'm immune — you don't bother me."

"Too bad."

Holly swung around to face him. "You mean you want to bother me?"

Steve laughed. "I like to get a rise out of you."

"Thanks a lot. Just what I need when I'm playing tennis."

"Then I do bother you?"

"Oh, go away, will you? Go bother someone else."

Steve turned to go, but then he stopped and said, "Only under protest. I like to watch you play. You look pretty."

Holly shook her head in exasperation. Of course he was only teasing her, yet she felt cheered. She served an ace as soon as he left. Before she served again, she stopped to watch him walk up the hill to the tents and wondered whatever was going on in his head.

At rest hour that day, after lunch, Holly stretched out on her back on her bed. She was staring up at the ceiling when Penny climbed up alongside her. "You look sad." The small girl patted her gently. "Don't look sad."

"Sometimes people feel sad. It's not terrible. After a while it goes away."

"But I don't like it. It makes me feel sad, too. Do you want to cry?"

Holly smiled at her. "No, I don't want to cry. I don't feel that sad. I feel more thinking-sad, not crying-sad. Maybe I'm homesick."

"I'm not homesick anymore. I was in the beginning. I like it here. Don't you?"

"Yes, I like it very much."

"I like you and Steve best." Penny hugged her.

Holly was surprised. "I didn't know you liked Steve."

"Well, I do. He's very nice. I like him because he likes you. Do you love him?"

Holly sat up to face Penny. "Where did you get such an idea? I like him, but I like a lot of people. I certainly don't love him and I doubt he likes me particularly. You shouldn't say things like that."

"I didn't think it was a bad thing to say." Penny looked hurt. "I won't like him if you don't want me to."

"You can like anyone you want. Don't like anyone for my sake. If you get your cards I'll play a game with you." Holly had had enough of talking about Steve.

Still later that day, after swimming, when Holly had a free hour or two, she felt that she had to go off someplace by herself. She had to pull herself together and get out of the situation dragging her down. First of all, Steve had another girl he was crazy about, and even if he didn't he was the last person in the world she should fall for.

Holly told Melissa she was going for a walk and struck off into the woods. She walked along a trail at a steady pace, and the steady physical action together with the silence of the forest calmed her nerves. There was no doubt in her mind that if she continued to let herself think about Steve she was headed for trouble. Liking him a lot could only hurt her. Yet, to be totally honest with herself, she had to face the fact that she was strongly attracted to him.

85

She was constantly aware of his presence, constantly reacting to him. His attitude could infuriate her, yet to be with him—even to argue with him—was becoming one of her great pleasures. It was an intolerable situation. She decided that "I'm Gonna Wash That Man Right Out of My Hair" should be her theme song.

Holly walked and walked. She left the trail and climbed onto a high rock. She stretched out and must have dozed off, because when she came to with a start it was getting on toward dusk. Holly jumped up. She'd better hurry up back to camp before it got dark. She looked around to decide from which direction she had come, in order to get herself back to the trail; but all the trees looked alike. With a growing panic she tried to remember where the sun had been when she came to the rock. First she was sure it had been to her right, and then positive it had been to her left.

Still undecided, but feeling she had to do something, she climbed down from the rock and headed out in the direction she thought might be right. But she took the precaution of marking her trail with strips torn from the bandanna she'd been wearing so that she could find her way back to the rock if she had to. After going quite a way with no sign of the main trail she turned back. She would have to try a different direction. Using the big rock as a center point, Holly fanned out three times with no success. By her fourth try it was getting dark, she had only a few of her bandanna strips left, and she was truly frightened. She was in the midst of probably thousands of acres of forest, and it was easy to get lost. What a fool she had been to have left the trail!

She stumbled along through the brambles and woods thinking what a stupid way for an independent, supposedly self-sufficient girl to die. Wouldn't Steve have the last laugh. In her anxiety and haste she had fallen a few times and her bare legs and arms were scratched and bloody, and she knew she had blood on her face from squishing some juicy mosquitos. Thinking of herself as independent and self-sufficient made Holly pull herself together and try to control her panic.

"I mustn't think about dying . . . Melissa knows I went for a walk, she'll miss me, and the camp will send scouts out to look for me . . . I must keep calm and not panic . . . I must . . . I must . . ." Yet the thought of being in the forest, alone in the dark, was not comforting. She was dangerously close to tears, when suddenly she saw a little clearing ahead. She ran toward it and in her excitement — she fell onto the trail. For minutes she didn't get up. She simply sat and let the tears run down her cheeks, sobbing with relief. After a while she picked herself up and walked briskly along the trail. She didn't have a watch on, but it was getting so dark she was sure she must have missed supper, but she didn't care. If she went down to the kitchen Joe would give her something to eat. Besides, nothing mattered now that knew she wasn't going to spend the night alone in the woods. She felt so good that it was easy to forget how terrified she had been only a short while before.

She was walking along, singing aloud, happy to

see the lights from camp flickering not too far away. Suddenly a figure emerged out of the darkness walking toward her. She was startled, then frightened, then surprised: Steve was striding toward her. His voice was accusing when he caught up with her. "What are you singing about? You had everyone worried sick. Where the devil have you been?"

"I went out for a walk. I went off the trail and for a while couldn't find my way back. I'm sorry if I gave anyone any trouble."

"You should *never* go off the trail in these woods. Do you realize that people can get lost here easily, and die? Of all the stupid, idiotic things to do!" His face was scowling as he walked alongside her. "I don't suppose you even had sense enough to be frightened."

"I *was* frightened. I was scared stiff until I found the trail again. I wasn't having a good time." She felt close to tears again.

Her tone and admission mollified him. "I don't imagine you were. You really had us all worried." His voice was kinder.

"I didn't expect you to worry about me. It was nice of you to come look for me."

"Mrs. Miller asked me to," he said gruffly. "This forest is no place for a girl alone at night."

"Would it be any better for a boy?" Holly asked innocently.

"Do you always have to bring that up? Yes, it *would* be easier for a boy, but a boy would have more sense than to go off by himself and then leave the trail. A boy wouldn't be so dumb."

"Thanks a lot." She tried to walk ahead of him

but he kept right alongside of her. She could feel her blood boiling. All the frustration of the past few hours, and the anguish and ambivalence of the past few days, were coming to a head in a fierce anger. How could she ever have imagined that she was in love with this arrogant, smug, impossible boy?

"I hate you," she yelled at him. "You are the most self-satisfied, stupid, ignorant person I have ever known. I feel sorry for any girl who has anything to do with you. She'd have to be a half-wit in the first place to bother!"

"Well, now you've gotten that out of your system, you feel better?" he asked quietly.

"Oh, don't you patronize me. Don't you dare. How I feel is none of your business," she added furiously. But she felt inadequate, enraged that he seemed to be mocking her, standing by so calmly as if she were the proverbial hysterical female. Again she felt an overwhelming desire for physical contact, to hit him, to wrestle with him, and — she realized suddenly — to have him take her in his arms and comfort her. I must really be crazy, she thought.

They walked into camp in silence. The Rectangle was quiet since almost everyone was in the social hall. Holly could hear their voices and music. "You missed supper," Steve said. "If you go down to the kitchen Joe'll give you something to eat."

"I'm not hungry, thank you."

Steve shrugged. "See you around."

Holly, of course, was starving. She watched Steve go up the hill and wondered if she could get into the kitchen without his seeing her. She didn't know why she had said she wasn't hungry. But that wasn't true either; she did know why. Steve turned her completely around. Never had she been so attracted to someone and hated him at the same time. She felt as if there were a constant war going on within herself, that her mind was telling her one thing — forget Steve Jackson — and her emotions saying the opposite. Her emotions frightened her. Holly was a normal, healthy girl; she'd been kissed by boys a few times in her life but she had never allowed intimacy to go beyond closeness and kissing nor had she ever wanted it to. But Steve's presence was making her aware of new feelings. His habit of looking at her long and thoughtfully, as he did, gave rise to a hundred fantasies of intimacy between them. Holly felt that the chemistry between them was getting to be more than she could cope with. She was becoming emotionally exhausted.

With Steve out of sight, she went down to the kitchen. Joe's helpers were gone but he was still there, and with some good-natured grumbling, he made her a huge ham sandwich. Holly sat on a corner of the kitchen table eating it and downing a glass of milk. "Where you been?" Joe asked. "You're all scratched up."

Holly told him about her adventure. "Steve came and found me, but I was already on the trail. That was nice of Mrs. Miller to send him."

"Mrs. Miller?" The cook looked at her curiously. "She ain't here. She left this afternoon to go into Boston for some business. Must have been his own idea."

Holly was stunned. "I didn't even thank him," she murmured.

"He won't mind. I knew him when he was a little kid coming here to camp, a good kid, Steve. Always polite, never no rough stuff. He likes to do things for people."

"Does he?" Holly was examining the apple Joe had handed her, but her mind was on the unfathomable expression in Steve's eyes when he looked at her.

olly watched the girls in the bunk make their beds, as they did every morning, and wondered about them: Were they going to grow up to be housewives for men like Steve or would they be doing exciting things in science, engineering, or maybe medicine? A month or two ago, before she came to Camp Lillinonah, she would have been sure. She would have been positive that there was a whole new world ahead for girls like herself, growing up, but now she wasn't so optimistic. Her confidence was rocked by her own feelings: how could a girl with her convictions be so *ordinary*, so boy-silly (as she put it to Melissa), as to be thrown by someone like Steve? She felt she had betrayed herself.

Holly was worried. The following weekend was parents' weekend. Her parents were coming up and so were Steve's. And Steve's parents were bringing his girl Nancy. Holly didn't know how she would get through the weekend. She would love to disappear, but she was also very eager to see her parents — yet even that had its drawbacks. She was aching to talk to her mother, but her mother, with her all-seeing eye, would worm things out of her that she wasn't ready to talk about.

"Honest to God," Holly said to Melissa, "life certainly is weird." She was laughing but her eyes were serious. "I came up here thinking I was getting away from problems at home, but I've gotten into a worse mess here. If this is what my mother calls 'getting interested in boys,' I'd just as soon not."

"Maybe you're not as strong on women's rights and independence as you thought you were," Melissa said. They were in Melissa's arts and crafts room watching the children make baskets to show to their parents.

"No, it's not that. I feel stronger about it than ever — Steve makes me even more sure of it. It's just that . . ." She hesitated. "I wonder how things will change, if they ever do. My mother gave up a good job because she didn't want to hurt my father, because she loves him. Steve's girl is his girl because she must make him feel good, the big superior male. There must be millions of boys like that. See what I mean? What good is all our talk if the boys still want cuddly dolls? It makes me wonder . . . how will I ever find a man I can honestly love without hating myself?"

"Maybe the boys will change. Not *everyone* is like Steve."

"I wish he was mean and nasty. I wish he wasn't so attractive." Holly picked up a small hammer from Melissa's work table and fiercely began to drive a nail through a piece of wood.

The closer the weekend drew near, the more Holly dreaded it. That Steve's girl was coming with his parents made her feel worse. As if they were practically engaged, Holly told herself. She tried to console herself with the knowledge that in a few weeks the summer would be over. Steve would be going home to Philadelphia and she'd be going home to Brookline. She'd never have to see him again. But somehow that thought wasn't altogether as comforting as she would have liked.

On the Wednesday before the weekend, Steve asked her at lunch time if she would go out in a canoe with him after supper. She was speechless with surprise. When she recovered herself, she said drily, "To drown me, I suppose?"

"Don't think I haven't thought of it," he answered, equally deadpan. "Are you game?"

"But of course. I'm a good swimmer and wildly curious. Do you think a canoe is big enough to hold both of us?"

"I'm counting on the fact that a canoe may be the one place where you can't slug me."

"Mmm, that's an interesting thought. Slugging you, I mean."

"Meet me at the boathouse right after supper," Steve said.

"Got it," Holly told him.

That afternoon was probably the longest one she

had spent in her life. During rest hour after lunch she tried reading, but that soon proved impossible. Why on earth did Steve invite her to go out in a canoe with him? And now, of all times, the weekend before his parents and girl were coming up? He must have something he wanted to talk to her about—but what? Wild fantasies raced through her head: He was going to tell her that he was going to be married or that he was already secretly married, or perhaps he just needed to talk to someone about how much in love he was. But why pick on her? Why Holly?

The afternoon dragged on. Down at the lake for swimming period he was there but paid no attention to her. She could have been a ripple in the water. Up at the tennis court he walked by but seemed lost in thought.

Before supper Holly took a shower, put on a clean pullover and shorts, and brushed her hair vigorously. Over the summer she had acquired a becoming, even tan, and the sun had brought out interesting red glints in her hair. Her muscles had hardened, and it seemed to Holly her legs had lengthened by at least a couple of inches. She was looking her best, she thought, examining herself in the mirror, better than she had ever looked in her life. She never used more than a bit of eye shadow for makeup, and she applied that now carefully. With a sigh, she gave herself one last look in the mirror before she turned to go out. She felt as if she had gotten dressed up to go to a funeral.

Although supper that night was one of her favorites, roast beef and hashed brown potatoes, Holly didn't eat much. Very often announcements were made after everyone was served dessert, and that evening was no exception. Holly thought the speeches would never end; it seemed that everyone had to say something. Mr. Miller made some remarks, then Mrs. Miller, and then Steve got up to make announcements about programs. He was his usual confident, relaxed self, cracking a few jokes that made everyone laugh. Holly thought that he, too, never looked better. His thick, longish hair was wet and brushed, and his blue shirt was exactly the right color for his eyes. Obviously, though, taking her out in a canoe was no big deal for him, and his calm nonchalance made her nervous excitement seem stupid.

When, finally, everyone got up from their tables, Holly did not rush down to the lake. She didn't want to get there before Steve did, so she sauntered along slowly. When she saw him stop in The Rectangle to talk to some of the kids, she deliberately went down to her bunk and waited there for five or ten minutes. When she came out she didn't see him, so she walked as slowly as she could down to the boathouse. He was waiting there for her.

"Sorry if I'm late," she greeted him.

"That's all right," he said cheerfully. "Girls are always late."

She didn't say anything but she gave him a look that told him what she thought of that remark. Steve laughed. "Okay. Some girls are late some of the time —"

"— but a foolish boy is foolish all of the time," Holly finished for him.

"Touché." Steve grinned.

They picked out a canoe that Steve said had no leaks and pulled it into the water. It had been a very hot day even for August, and the air had turned heavy and muggy. Thunderstorm weather, Holly thought, but she kept the thought to herself because she didn't want to turn back to obey the camp rule of not being on the lake in a storm.

They paddled well together and moved out across the lake easily. Steve, at stern, headed them into a finger of the lake almost opposite camp. The water was a dead calm, and Steve suggested that they pull in their paddles and drift along the shore. Holly did as he said and then turned around and sat in the bottom of the boat, facing him. "So, what's on your mind?" she asked.

"What makes you think I have anything special on my mind?" He grinned down at her.

"I'm not the kind of girl you would ask out on the lake. I'm not your type." She, too, had a smile on her face.

"Didn't think you'd ever admit you were a type," he murmured. Before she could answer, he leaned forward and continued. "As a matter of fact, there are some things I'd like to talk about."

Holly leaned back against the bow seat and stretched out her legs. "Okay, shoot."

"Well . . ." Steve shifted uneasily. "You know that my girlfriend Nancy is coming up this weekend with my folks. I want it to be a good weekend. Your parents are coming, too, aren't they?" Holly nodded. "I guess I just wanted to make sure we wouldn't be hassling each other." He looked down to meet her eyes.

"I don't mind no hassling for the weekend, but why tell me this? You'll be busy with your folks and your girl, and I'll be busy with my parents. We probably won't even see each other."

"That's just the point. I'd like us all to be friends. I want you to meet Nancy. I hope you two will like each other. I'd like to meet your folks and have you meet mine." Steve was very serious. "Maybe we could even do something together."

Holly stared at him with true surprise. "Why should we all be friends?" She leaned toward him suspiciously. "Say, are you trying to use me? Do you want me around to make your Nancy jealous? Her summer competition or something?"

Steve shook his head vigorously. "Nothing like that. I don't have to make her jealous — we get along fine. I just thought it would be nice for everyone to be friendly and to get together. Maybe it's foolish. Forget it. Sorry I brought it up."

"No, it's okay." Holly looked at him curiously. "Sometimes you can be so nice. You really like everyone to get along, don't you?" She sighed. "You have such a pretty picture of the world. Everything's super: Men have their place, women have theirs, and everyone's happy. It must be nice to be so naive, really sweet. I'm not being sarcastic, I mean it."

"You make me sound pretty sappy. But don't you want people to be friends with each other? I mean those you like?"

Holly leaned back and trailed her hands in the water. The sky was darkening with a blanket of clouds, blurring the outline of the camp buildings on the shore opposite. She felt that they should be turning back before the storm hit them, but it was nice, although eerie, being there with Steve, as if they were being wrapped up together in a cocoon of mist and growing darkness. It would be exciting to be on the lake in a storm. "I suppose so," she answered. "It's nothing I've ever thought about. I doubt that Nancy will like me. From what you've said, she has completely different ideas about what a girl should be."

"I didn't expect you to be palsy-walsy. I meant just that we'd all get along."

Holly sat up straighter. "What are you afraid of? Did you expect a hair-pulling match or something? Honestly, Steve, to tell you the truth, I don't really care about Nancy and I'm not terribly interested in making friends with her, even for a weekend. She sounds like a drip to me."

"There you go. Just because she's someone who thinks differently than you, you put her down before you even meet her. I might have known." Steve was angry.

Holly laughed. "This is crazy. Why are we arguing about someone I don't even know and who isn't here?"

"We argue about everything," Steve said ruefully.

They were both startled by a loud clap of thunder. In seconds the sky had turned black. "We'd better go back," Holly said. "It's going to pour any minute."

"No." Steve shook his head. "There's not enough time to get back to camp, and water's the worst place to be in a thunderstorm. This lake especially, it can get wild."

"What do you want to do?" Holly liked storms. She thought they were dramatic and exciting. "We could just stay here."

"No, we have to pull into shore. We can find a big rock to get under. That would be the safest." Steve was busy steering the canoe into the cove of an island, but his movements were jerky and the canoe rocked from side to side.

"Hey, what are you doing?" Holly was laughing.

"Just trying to get in in a hurry. You could help, you know." Steve got out of the boat and was pushing it up to the shore.

"Okay, okay. But what's the rush? It's not even raining yet." There was another loud clap of thunder and a streak of lightning across the sky.

"That one was nearer," Steve said.

Holly shot him a look and it occurred to her that he was nervous about the storm, but she didn't say anything. She helped him pull up the boat and turn it over, and then followed him up over some rocks into the woods. "We shouldn't be under trees," Steve said, stopping for breath. "There are some big rocks around here that make kind of a cave. I hope I can find them."

"We'll be all right even if you don't," Holly said, but she continued to follow him as he went one way and then another through the brush and trees, climbing up and down steep grades. In his hurry he stumbled and almost fell a couple of times.

"Hooray!" Steve called finally, a little way ahead of her. "Come on, we can crawl in here." He was crouching under a small mass of rocks, one with an overhang of a few feet. There really wasn't enough room for two people, and Holly said that she was all right under the trees. But Steve insisted. He pulled her in beside him and they sat close together under the rocks.

The thunder was coming more frequently now, in loud, rolling claps, and each burst was accompanied by brilliant streaks of lightning. Then suddenly the rain came down in a torrent. Holly huddled closer to Steve, and each time the thunder came she could feel a tremor go through his body. "You okay?" she asked.

Steve didn't answer. She could feel him trembling. Then, with an especially violent clap of thunder, he turned and put his face against her shoulder. "I'm not okay," he mumbled. "I'm terrible."

Holly put her arm around him. "Close your eyes, keep your head down. Don't look at it." She realized that he was terrified.

After a few minutes Steve lifted his face. "I can imagine what you're thinking. Why did this have to happen, and with you, of all people! I feel like such an idiot."

"Don't. It's okay. Lots of people are afraid of thunderstorms. It's nothing to be ashamed of. They can be scary."

"You're not afraid. I shouldn't be. I know riding in a car is a lot more dangerous. But ever since I was a kid, I've been terrified. My mother thinks it's because when I was little, not even three, we were caught in a sailboat in a big storm."

"That could be it," Holly said.

Steve grabbed hold of her with another loud clap of thunder. "No, I don't think it's that," he said when he recovered. "I think it's more complicated. I've never talked about this to anyone before, but I honestly think it's because of the way I am. I like to be in control, to be in charge. It's what you hate about me. In a thunderstorm I'm completely out of control, I'm at the mercy of the elements. I don't like that."

Holly turned around to look into his face and she knew he was in deadly earnest. "I don't hate you," she said quietly. "I'm glad you can talk to me."

"You didn't laugh at me. You might have made fun of me—big macho Steve afraid of a storm. It was a perfect opportunity."

"It didn't occur to me. A decent person doesn't laugh at someone else's weakness, and I hope I'm decent."

"You are," Steve said. "But you must admit that knowing my weakness must make you feel pretty good."

"It makes me like you more, if that's what you mean. I'm relieved that you're *not* the perfect macho male."

With the next roll of thunder Steve kept his face up, close to hers, and held her hand tight. Then, suddenly, he had his arms around her and was kissing her full on the mouth. Holly didn't resist him.

When Steve pulled away he was flustered. "I'm sorry, I don't know what got into me."

Holly looked at him questioningly, and then she turned her eyes away. "It's all right," she said softly.

"I don't know if it's all right. Nancy's my girl, we've gone together since we were freshmen in high school. And as you've said a hundred times, you and

102

come from different places. Yet . . . I don't know . . ." He shook his head in bewilderment. "I'm all mixed up."

"You'll get unmixed when she's here. Forget about this, it was nothing. A friendly kiss, that's all. Remember, we're friends just for the summer."

"Is that how you feel about it?" Steve asked. She thought he sounded stiff.

"Yes, of course," Holly lied.

They sat out the storm and Holly could feel his body close to hers, but he did not put his arms around her again. Yet Holly felt closer to him than she had ever felt to anyone. She was happy and sad at the same time and wondered how that could be: happy that for those few moments he was close to her and that they had reached a deeper understanding, in spite of their differences. And sad realizing that she loved him and that he loved someone else. She felt as though in the space of a brief thunderstorm she had grown a hundred years, and that, too, was a sad kind of knowledge. It was painful, at sixteen, to find that because of who she was, a girl with a mind of her own and a will to be equal and independent, she would lose out in love. The other kind of girl, the Nancy kind, would be the one to get her man.

Like most summer storms this one was over soon, and when the rumbles of thunder were safely in the distance, Steve said he was okay and that they could leave. He took Holly by the hand to help her out of their cave and, still holding it, led her back to the boat.

Before getting into the canoe Holly tried to shake

some of the water out of her hair and her clothes. She could feel Steve's eyes on her, and with a final shake of her head she said, "I must look a mess."

"No," he said quietly, "you're like the ads say, all natural. No additives, no preservatives, nothing artificial added. It's nice."

"Yeah, like granola." She was deliberately flippant because the way he was looking at her made her wish he would kiss her again, and that was dangerous thinking. "Come on, let's go," she said and stepped into the boat.

They hardly spoke on the way home. After they docked the canoe and walked up from the boat house, Holly turned and said good night. Steve stopped her from walking away. "You know, I meant what I said, about hoping we could get together over the weekend. I'd really like to meet your parents — I don't mind admitting I'm curious."

"To see who could produce such a freak?" Holly smiled at him.

"Sure. Do they each have two heads?"

"Absolutely, you'll see. Seriously, let's just play it loose, okay? Let's just see what happens."

"Sure, if that's what you want." He seemed reluctant to let her go, but Holly said good night again, carelessly blew him a kiss, and walked down to her bunk.

That night she wrote in her journal: *If only I felt as laid back about Steve as I'm trying to act. Sitting there squished under those rocks with him clinging to me, afraid of the thunder, I had the strangest feeling. It was spooky. I felt that there had been a mix-up somewhere, that a mistake had been made,*

104

wires crossed. He shouldn't be with Nancy, he should be with me, we belong. But of course there's no such thing as fate being wrong. Fate is fate, and there's nothing to be done about it. Besides, it's all in my head, not his. Nancy is his type and I'm not. Unrequited love, boohoo. Only it's not funny.

10

There was still Thursday and most of Friday to live through before the bus arrived from Boston with the visitors. There was a motel not far from camp where most of the parents would stay, and Holly had reserved a room there for her mother and father. She wished she could move in and stay with them for the weekend instead of being around camp.

Ever since Wednesday she had been trying to figure Steve out. He kept looking at her as if there was something he wanted to say, yet when there was an opportunity to catch her alone, he avoided it. "Falling for a boy who only wants you to be a friend is bad enough," she said to Melissa, "but to have to see him every day all day is impossible. And on top of that to have to meet his girl . . . I'm not sure I can hack this weekend. And Steve of all people—the whole thing is crazy. He can get me so mad."

"He wouldn't get you mad if you didn't like him so much," Melissa said. "I thought that all along. But the summer will soon be over and you won't ever have to see him again."

"Yeah, I know." But the thought of not seeing Steve was as bad as seeing him. Also, it occurred to Holly that Melissa used to insist that Steve liked her, but she didn't say that anymore. That made it final. If she had any stupid hope that Steve might want her as his girl she'd better forget it. She wished she could hate him.

As early as breakfast on Friday the excitement in camp was visible. It was certainly audible in the noisier than usual voices of the children, which the counselors made little effort to quiet. Holly had been warned by the old-timers not to bother to do much that day since the kids would be too keyed up waiting for their parents to arrive.

It suited her fine to leave her girls alone. She had her own problems to think about. Holly, too, was excited about seeing her parents, but apprehensive about how she would find them. Her own distraction —thinking about Steve, his parents, and his girl— made her feel guilty about her mother and father. She wanted them to have a super kind of weekend, but she was worried that her own nervousness and downbeat feeling about Steve would spoil it. She realized that she had wanted to show off to them how well she had gotten along on her own, to have them meet the nice friends she had made, and to admire what she had accomplished with the girls in her bunk. Now she was afraid that her upset had set her back. In some ways the experience made her feel more grown-up than before, but she was also annoyed that a boy like Steve could throw her so much. She wished the weekend was over before it started.

By three o'clock, a good hour before the bus was expected, practically all of camp was up at the entrance, sitting on the grass waiting. Holly's group huddled around her. "Wait till my mother sees how I swim," Penny repeated for the fourth or fifth time. "And my parents see me play tennis," Sharon added.

"What are you going to show your mother?" Penny turned to Holly.

"I'm going to show my parents what a nice bunk I have," Holly said.

"I love you," Penny said. "I'm going to be sorry when camp is over." She gave her a hug and set about combing Holly's long hair, a pastime that Penny loved.

It was half past four when the bus filled with parents pulled into camp. A few driving their own cars had arrived earlier, but Holly's mother and father were on the bus. The three embraced each other with hugs and kisses, and then Mr. and Mrs. Swanson stood back to get a good look at Holly. Holly twirled around for them, conscious of her own glowing healthiness, but with a pang of guilt for their tired faces. She didn't dare ask her father how his business was; she could see on his face that it was no better.

While she was chatting with her parents and wondering if the camp truck was going to take their

108

luggage over to the motel, she kept looking around for Steve's parents and his Nancy. She saw him carrying suitcases over to the truck but he didn't seem to be with anyone. Then he came over to her. "Didn't your parents come?" Holly asked, suddenly a hope rising that maybe they hadn't.

"They're driving up. My father's a car freak, he insists on going on his own steam."

"I feel the same," Mr. Swanson said. "My wife's the one who wanted to try the bus."

Holly introduced them, and Steve shook hands with them both. "What does your father drive?" Mr. Swanson asked.

"Right now he's driving a Mercedes. Not a new one," Steve added hastily.

"Mmph," Mr. Swanson grunted. "Doesn't like American cars?"

"Oh no, it's not that. He just happened to get a good buy from a friend." Steve gave him a friendly smile.

"That's what makes it tough for the dealers," Mr. Swanson remarked.

"Don't you want to go over to the motel and freshen up?" Holly asked quickly, anxious to change the subject. She could see Steve's hope of their all getting together fading rapidly.

"Yes," her mother said. "Can we walk?"

"I think so." Holly turned to Steve. "Will the truck bring over their suitcases?"

"Yep. I'm driving it over myself. See you there."

Holly led her parents back to the road to the motel. "I'll show you all around camp later when we go back," she said.

"Your friend seems like a nice boy. Very good-looking," her mother commented.

"A Mercedes, even a used one, is not a cheap car," her father muttered.

"Steve's okay," Holly said casually. "He's no millionaire, though, Pop, don't worry."

Her mother gave her a curious look. "Is he the one you told me about, the one who gives you such a hard time?"

"We've gotten over that. We're friends now. As a matter of fact, he wants us to get together, the three of us, with his parents and his girl."

"His girl?" Her mother sounded surprised. "Does he have a girl here?"

"She's coming up with his parents." Holly gave her mother a swift warning glance. But in spite of all her casualness, Holly was sure that her mother, with her sensitive antennae, was aware that things were more complicated than they seemed.

The motel room was comfortable, one of a row with verandas that faced the lake. In a short while Steve drove up and brought in the suitcases. "Well, what do you know," he said. "My folks and Nancy are just next door. You have 104 and they have 106 and 108. The way these porches run together we can have a party." He looked at Holly with a mischievous grin.

He's enjoying this, she thought angrily. He can't wait to have the two of us together, his *girl* friend and his girl *friend* — oh, I could kill him, I could really kill him. Yet, she had to admit ruefully, the situation was amusing and full of intrigue. She would

110

have loved to be in Steve's position: to have a boy-friend arrive who was madly in love with her and to pitch him against Steve. What a time she would have had.

Aloud she said to Steve, "We don't plan to spend much time over here. My parents will be at camp except to sleep."

"No doubt," Steve said with an ingratiating smile.

As it turned out, Holly and her parents were sitting on their veranda when the car with the Jacksons and Nancy arrived; they had evidently stopped at camp first to get Steve since he was with them. Holly's first impression of Nancy was that she was very pretty, her legs were too skinny, and that she should never have gotten such a curly perm. Yet, after the introductions had been made and the two families were sitting together outdoors, Holly felt unexpectedly at ease. Having finally met Nancy was a relief. Her style was so totally different from Holly's, it made any connection between herself and Steve seem totally improbable.

As Holly said later to Melissa, "If he could be serious about a girl like Nancy, then he could never really like me. Not that she isn't nice," she had added. "She's perfectly all right, and she adores Steve. If he told her to jump into the lake she'd do it. If he wants someone who looks up to him and will cater to him, he's got it."

Nancy's attitude became apparent very quickly. While the parents were chatting, Mr. Jackson remarked that he was thirsty. "I'll get you some water," Nancy said, jumping up to go inside.

111

"I'll go get it," Mrs. Jackson said at the same time and started to get up from the lounge chair she was in.

Steve looked from one to the other of them with a trace of annoyance on his face. "What are you two going to do, fight about who's going to get him a glass of water? Can't he get it for himself?"

Mrs. Jackson laughed. "Why Steve, who's been teaching you this summer?"

Holly shot him a quick, amused look that made him flush.

"Don't give your mother ideas," his father said good-naturedly. "I'm happy with the way things are."

"I'll get the water," Nancy said, and vanished inside to return with a filled glass. "Here." She handed the glass to Mr. Jackson. "I'll wait on you any time," she said cheerfully. She went over to Steve and put her arm through his possessively. "And you, too," she said softly.

Holly thought Steve was embarrassed, although he was trying to hide it. "There's time for a swim before we go back to camp for supper. You want to?" he asked Nancy.

She touched her hair and shook her head. "I don't want to get my hair wet now, it'll take ages to dry. I'd rather wait until tomorrow when the sun's hot. But of course if you really want me to. . . ?"

Steve shrugged. "It's not important."

Holly felt the silence to be thundering. She finally broke it. "Let's go back to camp," she said to her parents, "and I'll show you around." She felt that another minute of watching Steve's bored face would

112

make her say or do something foolish. If he had any brains, she thought, he'd go off someplace to be alone with his girlfriend. She wondered why he wasn't doing it.

Steve jumped up when she spoke. "You want me to drive you?"

"I don't think so. We can walk." Holly looked to her parents and they nodded agreement.

On the road Mr. Swanson walked ahead and Holly and her mother followed more slowly, arm in arm. "Your friend doesn't look too happy with his girl," her mother said.

"It's probably because his parents are around," Holly said lightly.

"Maybe," Mrs. Swanson said. She turned to face Holly. "You like him a lot, don't you?"

Holly twisted her hair around her fingers with her free arm. "I told you we were just friends. I'll never see him again after this summer anyway. He lives in Philadelphia."

"And of course there are no trains or buses," her mother murmured.

"Forget it, Mom. More important, tell me how you are. Anything new with Dad?"

Mrs. Swanson shook her head. "Not really. Not yet, anyway. The auto business is lousy, and he's thinking of giving it up. If he can raise some money I think he'd like to buy into a hardware business. Old Jack Penfield is in his sixties and wants to retire one of these days. He'd like Dad to come in and learn the business, and then he'd pull out gradually and turn it over to Dad."

"That sounds good. What's the hitch?"

"Money, darling. You need money to buy into a business."

"Wouldn't he get anything for his dealership? For the store?"

"I'm afraid not much. Who wants to buy a business that's on the skids?"

"There's got to be some way," Holly said. "Couldn't you mortgage the house?"

Her mother smiled. "We already have as much of a mortgage as we can handle. You're a good kid, Holly. Don't you worry about it, we'll figure out something."

"Why shouldn't I worry about it? I'm part of this family," Holly said. "I'm not a kid anymore. I'm sixteen, and I'll be seventeen soon. Maybe I should quit school and get a job?"

"Absolutely not," her mother said firmly. "Your education money is in the bank. Don't even think about that."

Holly walked her parents around camp, showing them the ball fields and tennis courts, the various buildings, and the lakefront, until the gong rang for supper. The usual table seating by bunks had been abandoned so that the children could eat with their parents, and Holly looked around for a place where she and her parents could sit together. Steve and his group were at a table that had three empty places, and he got up and motioned to her to join them. Though it was not what Holly wanted, there was no polite way to refuse. But it didn't work out too badly. Her father and Mr. Jackson soon got to talking the economy and business, while Mrs. Jackson

114

seemed very interested in Mrs. Swanson's business career.

Holly learned that Nancy was at the same community college as Steve and, like him, had finished her first year. "But I'm thinking of changing," Steve said. "I've got applications in at several schools, including Boston U." He glanced at Holly. "I'd rather be at a good university."

"Harwinton Junior College is good enough for me," Nancy said. "I'm not looking for a career anyway."

"What do you plan to do?" Holly asked politely.

Nancy laughed. "Get married and have babies, I suppose. That will keep me busy. Don't you think so?" The question was directed at Steve.

"If that's all you want to do," he said.

Nancy raised her eyebrows in surprise. "You always thought that was what a woman *should* do." She turned to Holly with a confidential smile. "You should hear him carry on about women and careers."

"I have heard him," Holly murmured. "You haven't changed your mind, have you?" She turned to Steve with an innocent face.

"How'd we get on this subject anyway? Whether you like it or not, I'm taking you out on the lake after supper," he said to Nancy, cutting off that conversation.

"I'll like it," Nancy said placidly.

Of course you will, Holly thought. You'll like whatever he tells you to like.

From The Rectangle she watched them go down to the boathouse and take out a canoe. For all her

115

exterior calm, she was hurting. Holly wondered if he would take her to the island, their island, where they had kissed under the big rocks. She didn't want to think about that; it hurt too much. Yet she did keep thinking about it, and wishing that she had known before all she had learned during that thunderstorm: that a person, a girl *or* a boy, can be soft and gentle and yet be strong. If she could only remember that. Sitting with Steve that day, she had learned that his manhood had not been diminished by his fear, nor had she relinquished the strength of her feminism by giving him gentleness and comfort. Her mother knew that. Her mother knew how to be caring and loving and still be strong. Strong enough to put her husband's needs ahead of her own when it seemed necessary. Holly felt ashamed that she had been so righteous in condemning her mother for renouncing principles. Holly gave a deep sigh. To be a woman was not easy — not "Superwoman," she never wanted to be that — but to be tender and generous, and strong and equal.

Her mother walked over to her and put her arm around her shoulder. Holly could see her father sitting on the porch of the dining hall still in conversation with Mr. Jackson. Mrs. Jackson was nowhere in sight. "You look very pensive," her mother said, following Holly's eyes to the canoe on the water.

"I've been thinking. You know, you were right about not taking that job in White Plains. It would have finished Dad."

"Whatever made you think of that now?" Mrs. Swanson motioned toward the lake. "I thought you had other things on your mind."

116

"They're connected," Holly said. "I've decided that I'll never get along with boys, certainly not have a real relationship with a boy, if I go on the way I have. I mean, you can't continually put a boy down, and examine everything he says and does to be sure he's not putting you down. That kills everything from the start and you never get past it. You know what I mean?"

"I certainly do. You've done a lot of growing up this summer. Has Steve had anything to do with it?"

Holly nodded. "I guess so. We've been at each other like crazy, and perhaps we could have really liked each other, gotten close, if we hadn't made this mountain between us."

"But I thought you said that you did think differently, that he liked a girl to be, well, for lack of a better word, old-fashioned. That's not you."

"I know, I know. And I don't want to be that kind of girl either. But I didn't have to push down his throat the kind of girl I am — I came on like a bulldozer. I don't mean I want to be a hypocrite or put on an act, I mean just to be more giving. To be like you are."

Her mother threw her arms around her. "Why, Holly, that's the nicest thing anyone ever said to me. Thank you."

"Well it's true," Holly said.

117

11

Holly's parents got a ride back to the motel with the Jacksons, and they left before Steve and Nancy came in from the lake. Holly didn't want to be around when the canoe came in, so she went down to her bunk, and for lack of anything better to do got into bed. Her girls were already in bed and asleep after the excitement of the day.

But Holly couldn't sleep. She kept thinking of Steve and Nancy. Were they making love? How far did their lovemaking go? Nancy was an "old-fashioned" girl, but she was very eager to please Steve. They were both older than Holly, yet Holly felt that when it came to sex Nancy would be standoffish and prim. Holly's mind kept going round and round with images of Nancy and Steve in each other's arms, and then, out of the blue, her own face would be there instead of Nancy's.

Finally she couldn't stand it anymore. She kicked off her light blanket and looked at her watch. It was just after midnight. Surely they were back by now and it would be safe to go out. As quietly as possible she pulled on a pair of jeans and a shirt and went outside. It was almost as light as day. The full moon was brilliant and the sky was lit up with hundreds of stars. Holly wondered what it would be like to live alone in the woods with this bright stillness. But then she remembered the time she was lost and knew it would be different from pretty moonlight and a sleeping camp.

From The Rectangle she could see a swathe of moonlight across the lake, and she walked toward it. But she stopped before she got down to the beach when she saw that someone was sitting on one of the rocks. She didn't feel like running into anyone and turned to go in another direction, but a voice called out softly, "Hey, is that you, Holly?"

She recognized Pee-Wee's voice. "Yes. Are you all right?"

"Sure. Come over and sit down." He moved so that there would be room for her on the big flat rock. "What brings you out in the middle of the night?" he asked after she had joined him.

"I could ask you the same question. But isn't it beautiful?" she said, looking at the light on the water. "I couldn't sleep, that's all," she said after a minute or two.

"Me neither. The summer's going to be over soon, and I'm beginning to get jittery."

"What about?"

"I don't like ends and beginnings. I couldn't wait till I got out of high school, and now I'm out I have to face going to college. I'm going to a big university, Penn U., and it makes me nervous. I'm a small-town hick."

"Not you, you're smooth, Pee-Wee."

"Don't be taken in by my glamorous personality. I'm a failure. I've been trying to make you notice me all summer and you wouldn't give me a tumble. You can't dispute that." He was only half joking.

"That's not fair. Don't lay your mood on me. I like you very much, you know that. I'm not going to feel guilty because you couldn't get to sleep tonight." She gave him an indulgent smile.

"I think that's downright mean. What's a little guilt going to hurt you? It's good for your soul."

Holly laughed. "Listen, right now my soul's so loaded down I couldn't carry another ounce. I feel guilty about my parents, about not earning more money, about being . . . too dogmatic in my beliefs. I don't mean to change them but just not to come on so strong, to be more . . . well, like Steve's girl Nancy."

Pee-Wee gave her a sharp look. "You're worth a million Nancys. You don't want to be like her."

"Why not? Steve's crazy about her. That girl's going to get everything she wants in this world, and I won't."

"Don't you believe it. Just look at what she wants. Steve would get bored with her in no time."

"He hasn't so far."

"But you don't want what she wants," Pee-Wee

said. He kept looking at her as if he wanted to get a particular answer from her.

"Yes, I know . . ." Holly looked away, back to the water. "There are other people besides Steve," Pee-Wee said softly. "Not every boy thinks the way he does."

"Yes, I know," she repeated. She turned her head to meet Pee-Wee's eyes. "That's my trouble. I thought I could do everything. I thought I could change Steve, but it doesn't work that way. The only person you can change is yourself, isn't it?"

Pee-Wee nodded. They heard a sound and looked up to see Steve walking down toward them. "Probably just came back from taking Nancy to the motel."

"It's awfully late," Holly murmured.

Steve stood looking down at the two of them sprawled on the rock. He was obviously embarrassed. "I didn't mean to interrupt you. I just wanted to see who was down here."

"Why?" Pee-Wee asked coolly.

Steve shifted from one foot to the other uneasily. "To make sure everything was all right."

"Come on, you were curious, weren't you?"

Steve looked from one to the other. "Yeah. I was curious, so what? So now I know." He turned and started to walk away.

"You don't know nothin'," Pee-Wee called after him. "Don't jump to any conclusions."

"Thanks for the advice," Steve said curtly, and continued to walk up the hill toward the tents.

Holly stood up. "I'd better go in now. Are you coming?"

"Yeah, I guess so." Pee-Wee stood up too. "He didn't look very happy, did he? What's Steve got that I haven't got?"

Holly leaned over and gave him a kiss on the cheek. "It's just chemistry, love, that's what it's all about."

"No kidding. Funny, in my chem class they never taught me anything about that."

"Wait till you get to college, you'll learn."

They walked up the hill together and Pee-Wee left her outside her bunk. Holly got into bed for the second time that evening but it still took her a while to get to sleep. No, Steve had not looked very happy. She wondered how things were going between him and Nancy. Forget Steve, her common sense kept warning her. Forget him. He's not for you and he never would be even if there were no Nancy.

The next morning at breakfast Steve came over to her and said rather stiffly, "Our mothers want to go on a trip today and they want you and Nancy and me to go with them." He gave a slight smile. "They want me to do the driving. The men are going fishing."

"When was all this cooked up?" Holly asked in surprise.

"I guess last night. Mom told me when I brought Nancy back. You don't have to go if you don't want to," he added politely.

She didn't want to. To spend the day with Nancy and Steve — that was too much. "I'm afraid my mother would be hurt if I didn't," she said truthfully.

"After all, she came up here to see me. But what about camp? Can we both be gone all day?"

"Mrs. Miller said it was okay. There are enough counselors around, and it's an informal day anyway. A lot of the kids are going off on trips with their parents."

Holly shrugged. "Well, okay. What's the program? Where are we going?"

Steve looked amused. "Your enthusiasm is overwhelming. I don't know. I thought we could show them the Old Man in the Mountain, maybe drive to the foot of Mt. Washington. My idea was to play it by ear. They want to go to some fancy inn for lunch. Why don't I meet you in half an hour and we'll go over to the motel? I brought the car back here last night."

"Okay. I suppose I have to wear a skirt for one of those inns?"

"I dunno. Wear what you please."

Holly went back to her bunk and put on a denim skirt she had bought in the village and a dark purple tee shirt. She brushed her hair and put on a little eye makeup. Penny stood watching her. "You going out?"

"Yes, I'm going on a trip with my mother. What are you and your parents going to do?"

"I don't know. I'll show them how I can swim." Penny gave Holly a hug. "You look beautiful."

"Thank you." Holly kissed her. "You give me the best moral support."

"What does that mean?"

"That you make me feel good. Good-bye."

123

She met Steve outside and they walked up to the car in silence. Steve held the car door open for her. "You look pretty," he said.

"Thank you." She was dying to ask him if he was having a good weekend, but she didn't dare — it would be too obvious. "You didn't have to worry about our families getting together," she said brightly. "They seem to be hitting it off fantastically."

"Yeah, they do. Is it bothering you?"

"No, why should it?"

"I have the impression it's too cozy for you."

"I guess I'm surprised. I expected them to be too different to get along so well."

"People who are different *can* get along." He gave her a sidelong glance. "Or is that news to you?"

Holly made a grimace. "Lay off, Steve. Don't bait me. We have to spend the day together."

"You make it sound like a punishment."

She laughed gaily. "A fate worse than death."

Holly noticed immediately that Nancy had gone all-out to look her best. She was wearing a crisp white, mid-calf skirt and a sheer, embroidered blouse that revealed her figure provocatively. Her tanned legs were bare but she wore beige kid high-heeled pumps, and her makeup was applied expertly. Holly felt like a peasant beside her.

After their greetings, and after Nancy had gone back to her room twice — once to get her oversized sunglasses and then to make sure she'd pulled the plug on her hair dryer — they took off. As expected, Nancy sat in front with Steve and Holly in back with the two mothers. Holly resigned herself to having a terrible day. How, she wondered, had she ever gotten into this ridiculous situation: to be stuck for the day in a car with a boy she should dislike — but didn't — and his mother and his girlfriend. One day she would probably have a good laugh about it, but right now she wished she had woken up with a high fever that would have kept her in bed.

"This is so nice," her mother was saying to Mrs. Jackson. "It was lovely of you to ask us."

"It's my pleasure. Steve adores driving this car, and I didn't see any point in sitting around camp all day. This country is so beautiful."

It was easy for Holly to block out the conversation, what she called non-talk. No one was really saying anything, and Holly didn't expect that they would. Her own thoughts, however, were not that comforting. She tried to avoid looking at the two heads in front of her, Steve's and Nancy's, but her eyes kept going back to them. Every once in a while Nancy leaned over to say something to Steve in a low voice that Holly couldn't hear. She found herself getting angrier and angrier with Steve. He must have arranged all this with his stupid notion of everyone being friends. What was he trying to prove? In all fairness, however, she had to admit that he didn't know how painful this was to her. He didn't know that in spite of all their banter (or maybe because of it?) she had fallen in love with him. She was the one who had said friends just for the summer.

Steve drove them to various historic places. They looked at the Old Man in the Mountain; they walked through an eighteenth-century home; Holly and her mother and Steve climbed halfway up a mountain to look at a monument. Nancy and Mrs. Jackson stayed below, because of their shoes. Holly felt awkward and embarrassed when Steve said he would join her and and her mother, but Steve seemed perfectly at ease, and he chatted with her mother all the way. Holly could see that he was charming her.

"Are you having a good time?" he asked Holly on their way down.

"The scenery is beautiful," she said with a small smile. "What about you?"

"Interesting," he said with his amused look.

So far the most that Holly had heard Nancy say was, "I don't care." Whatever Steve suggested doing, that was her answer. Holly found herself waiting to hear it, and she wondered if everyone else was as conscious of that vapid response as she was. Holly vowed that never in her life, when she was asked what she wanted, would she answer, "I don't care."

It happened again at lunch. "What do you want to eat?" Steve asked.

"I don't care," Nancy said. "What are you having?"

"What difference does that make? You decide what you want." He sounded irritable.

"But I don't care," she said mildly. She looked at him with her big eyes. "I like to have you order for me."

"You probably won't like it. I'm having steak. I haven't had a good steak all summer. And french fries."

"That sounds fine. Probably more than I can eat, but that doesn't matter."

"It's silly," Steve mumbled, avoiding Holly's eyes.

Around four o'clock the mothers decided they were tired, and to Holly's relief Steve headed for home. He dropped his mother and Nancy and Mrs. Swanson at the motel and drove Holly back to camp. He would go back for the others later, when the men came in from fishing, and they would all come to camp for supper.

"Did you have a good time?" he asked Holly when they were in the car.

"You asked me that before. What difference does it make?"

Steve smiled. "I like to see people enjoy themselves."

"Did Nancy have a good time?"

"I didn't ask her."

"I don't see how she could, with your mother and two other females around. If I came up to see my boyfriend I wouldn't want to spend the day with a crowd."

"Nancy likes to do whatever I like. I told you she was very agreeable." He shot Holly a sidelong glance. "Not like some other people I know."

"Guess who? No, I am not like your friend Nancy, not one bit, and I don't want to be. But I think she suits you perfectly. 'Yes, Steve. No, Steve. I don't care, Steve.' " Holly's eyes were blazing. "She's a very nice girl. You should be very happy together."

"For Pete's sake. We're not getting married. We're not even engaged."

"You're not? If I were you I'd hang on to her. You're not apt to find many agreeable girls like that these days. She's one in a million." Holly didn't know why she was getting so angry. Perhaps because of spending the day with Nancy and Steve. She was disgusted with Nancy for playing up to Steve the way she did. To Holly that seemed the worst kind of sexism, and she was furious with Steve for falling for it. And she was angry with herself for caring.

She said good-bye to Steve abruptly and went off to her bunk. Before supper she wrote in her journal: *I am so mad. I'm letting Steve spoil my weekend with my parents. I'm as bad as Nancy, letting him manipulate me. I never should have gone with them today. I should have persuaded my mother to do something else. But then, I was curious to see him and Nancy together, like touching a sore spot. Well, I saw them, and it made me sick. Women will never get anywhere while there are still silly girls like Nancy around, and boys like Steve who eat it up. I don't mind if a girl wants to stay home and take care of her house and her kids, there's nothing wrong with that. It's Nancy's whole attitude to Steve — acting like he's so superior — that gets me. It's the last thing he needs. I don't know why I should give a darn, but I do.*

Holly was glad that in the evening the children put on a talent show, so there was no opportunity for socializing with the Jacksons. The camp and all the guests were packed into the social hall, and when the show was over everyone was tired. The Swansons went back to the motel with Steve's parents, but Holly noticed that Steve and Nancy were not with them. Later she saw them on the camp road walking back toward the motel. She ducked into her own bunk so they wouldn't see her, and resolutely she got undressed and into bed, determined not to think about Steve and his girlfriend Nancy.

12

Sunday morning Holly got herself excused from her breakfast duties and went over to the motel to be with her parents. Mrs. Swanson had decided she wanted to fix breakfast in their room and eat on the veranda. They were going to take an early bus home because Holly's mother had some work to do.

Holly thought that both her parents looked better than when they arrived. Especially her father. He had gotten a nice tan out fishing the day before, and he looked more his old self, not so downhearted. "Those Jacksons are nice people," he said to Holly. "The boy, too. A nice family."

Holly nodded politely. She was glad that they weren't next door now but had left to go over to camp. It was nice sitting outside with her parents, having a quiet meal after all the noisy camp ones. Her mother had borrowed a hot plate from the motel owner and fixed some wonderful eggs and bacon.

After breakfast Mr. Swanson said he didn't get much chance to walk in woods and that he was going for a short hike. When they were alone, Mrs. Swanson turned to Holly. "I've been doing a lot of thinking this weekend, and I got an idea. I'm not telling your father until I know if I can arrange it, so don't say anything."

"What, what?" Holly could tell that her mother was excited.

Mrs. Swanson leaned forward in her chair, and her eyes were bright. "I've been thinking that if I could take that job in White Plains for a limited time, get everything started and at the same time train someone to take over, perhaps I could make enough so that Dad could buy into the hardware store. What do you think? It would mean you'd have to help out during the week, cook dinners and all — I could only come home weekends."

"I think it's terrific. You've got to do it, Mom. The store's got to let you."

"I think maybe they would. They haven't found anyone else yet. And with some help from me, my assistant could handle things in Boston for a few months. But will be a load on you."

"I don't mind. I'll enjoy it. But, Mom . . ." Holly hesitated.

"What? What's the matter?"

"I'm glad you've changed your mind, but aren't you still worried that Dad will be upset at your doing

131

all this? I mean, you were so worried about his ego before."

"I've thought about that a great deal. But I think it's different now. First of all, this would be for a specific reason, something to get Dad back on his feet. It was different when he felt so hopeless. And it would only be for a relatively short time. Progress doesn't go in a straight line, darling. There are steps forward, and sometimes retreats, although I don't really think that not taking the job a couple of months ago was a retreat. You have to live what you believe in, that's true, but you can't be rigid and dogmatic. There has to be a give and take."

Holly looked at her mother thoughtfully. "You think I'm rigid?"

"Of course." Her mother smiled. "Most young people are, because they're idealistic. Old people have the reputation for being rigid, but I think it's the other way around, except for those who don't get any wiser as they get old. But most young people think life goes in a straight line, and they've got to stick to that line no matter what. They haven't learned yet how to be flexible. Try taking a shovel away from a kid in a sandbox. He yells it's unfair because it's his. Sure it's unfair, but it's also mean of him not to let anyone else use it."

Holly laughed. "I see what you mean. You're a smart lady."

Mrs. Swanson stood up and put their breakfast dishes on a tray. "I'm still learning, honey. And I hope I never stop." Holly stood up with her. "You're a nice girl, Holly," her mother said, "I'm proud of you. Don't let the retreats throw you."

"I'll try not to." Holly looked out thoughtfully over the lake before she followed her mother inside.

Later that morning Holly was at the bus station seeing her parents off. Mr. Jackson had offered to drive them, but Steve had insisted that he do it. He stood beside her as they watched the bus pull away. Steve seemed very quiet and preoccupied. "Do you want anything in town?" he asked.

Holly shook her head. "No, thank you. I'd better get back to camp."

"Is there a rush?"

"I have a swimming period at eleven."

"Yeah, that's right. I forgot."

Holly looked at him curiously. "That's a new twist. You forgetting the program."

"I'm not infallible," Steve said with a faint smile.

"I guess I thought you were. Are you all right?" He didn't look himself. Not sick, but strained, as if it was a big effort to pay attention.

"Sure. Or I should say kind of all right, not entirely. I've got some things on my mind."

They had been sitting in the car and now he turned on the motor and started driving. "These weekends can be pretty disruptive. The whole camp gets upset."

Holly wondered if he was talking about the camp or particularly about himself. But she didn't ask.

Holly felt depressed when she got back to camp. She had looked forward to spending the weekend with her parents, but she felt the time had gone by and they hadn't been together that much. Soon the summer would be over and she would have to say

133

good-bye to everyone, and Steve's downbeat mood hadn't helped. She wondered what he was so worried about, if he had had a fight with Nancy. But she didn't think Nancy was the kind who would fight.

Holly showed off to her girls' parents how well they could swim, but she was glad later in the afternoon to see the buses come in to pick up the parents and take them back to Boston. From Boston they would pick up their own transportation to go home. When the last bus pulled out, there was still some free time before supper, and Holly decided to take out a canoe.

Once she was on the lake she knew exactly where she wanted to go, and she headed for the island where she and Steve had sat out the thunderstorm. Going there, she suspected, was going to make her even more depressed, but she felt too tired to fight off her mood. She felt lethargic, almost welcoming an excuse to slide down into a good old-fashioned crying spell. What better place to indulge herself than under the big rock?

Holly beached the canoe and climbed through the brush and settled herself under the rock. She stretched out on her stomach, with her head buried in her arms, and her legs sticking out beyond the rock's shelter. She felt alone, and lonely, but no tears came.

She tried to empty her mind of all thought. She didn't want to think about her parents, or Steve and Nancy, or going home and back to school, or about her summer at the camp and the girls . . . Holly swung around and reversed her position, and turned over on to her back so that she could look up through the trees at the sky. Way up in the distance she could see a hawk flying and she concentrated on watching its graceful circling and the wide spread of its wings. She wondered if a hawk had feelings, if it could actually enjoy the beauty of its freedom. Holly hoped that it could.

She watched the sun slowly sink lower in the sky and knew that she should be getting back to camp for supper. But she figured that no one would miss her. They would probably think that she had gone somewhere with her parents, since their names were not on the list for the afternoon buses. Holly let herself drift into a pleasant limbo between sleeping and waking.

Suddenly, without opening her eyes, she felt someone's presence and she sat up with a start. Steve was standing over her. "Oh," she let out a cry. "You scared me!"

"I'm sorry. When I saw the canoe on the beach I was going to go away. Then I had a hunch that maybe you were here, so I came to see."

Holly stood up and brushed off her clothes. "Why did you come here?"

Steve picked up a small stone and aimed it at a tree several feet away. "I wanted to get away. To be alone, to think."

"Have your parents left?"

He nodded. "Yes." Then he looked directly into her eyes. "I broke off with Nancy," he announced. He said the words quietly, almost casually. It took a few minutes for them to sink in.

Holly simply stared at him. She felt her body go taut, as if someone were tightening the strings that held her together. She didn't know what to say.

"Aren't you going to say anything?" Steve asked after a few minutes. He had sat down on a rock and was nervously pulling up blades of grass.

"I don't know what to say. I'm sorry, I guess."

Steve looked up at her, standing opposite him, leaning against the big rock. He looked faintly amused. "Why should you be sorry?"

"I think it's always sad when a couple breaks up. One of them gets hurt."

"She'll get over it. Nancy won't be without a boyfriend for long."

"Then it was your idea?" Holly kicked a pebble with her foot. "You were so crazy about her . . . your kind of a girl."

"Stop saying that," Steve said irritably. "I'm only eighteen, don't put me in a box. I'm not the 'male chauvinist pig' you think I am. Besides, Nancy is probably the most boring girl in the whole of Pennsylvania, Massachusetts, and New Hampshire. I started counting up how many times she said 'I don't care' this weekend, but after around fifty I gave up."

Holly smiled, but she said tartly, "So after going together since you were freshmen, you gave her the gate. Just like that."

Steve picked up a stone and hurled it against a tree. "I don't believe you," he yelled. "You are impossible. You're going to find something wrong in everything I do. You don't want equality. You want superiority. You want to take a boy and step on him until he squirms. Don't you think Nancy would have

136

broken off with me if she had wanted to? You don't know anything about equality. It means the same for one as for the other. Was I supposed to hang on to Nancy out of pity, because she's a *girl?*"

"No, no, of course not. You're right. I'm sorry." She felt awful. Nothing she had said had expressed her feelings, the great elation she had felt when he told her he'd broken off with Nancy. As usual she had spoiled it all by jumping on him, putting him down. Exactly what she had made up her mind not to do anymore. But it wasn't so easy. It was going to take her years to learn. But for now everything was ruined.

"I guess I'd better go. You said you wanted to be alone." She glanced at him quickly and looked away. She felt as if she might burst into tears.

"Holly." Steve was up and he had his arms around her. "I'm crazy about you, don't you know that? You must know. My mom said it was written all over my face. Even Nancy guessed it." He was holding her tight and kissing her hair, her cheeks, her lips.

Holly let herself relax against him, and the tears streamed down her cheeks. "I don't know why I'm crying."

"I do," Steve murmured. "Because you've been wanting to give in as much as I have. You do care for me, don't you?"

"Yes, I do."

Steve held her until she stopped crying, and they sat close together on the rock. After a while Holly said, "The summer is almost over. Just for the summer, remember?"

"Oh no. There's Indian summer, and then summer in January . . . Some summers never end, they go on and on. My mother told me I was accepted at B.U. That means I'll be in Boston this year."

"Oh, Steve." She touched his cheek tenderly with her hand.

After a while they went down to the beach and there were the two canoes. Steve scratched his head. "I wish we could go back in one boat. This is silly, two separate canoes."

"No, it's okay. It's better."

Steve looked at her questioningly. "Better?" Then he laughed. "Separate but equal? Some fancy symbolism?"

Holly laughed, too. "Something like that." Then she turned to him with a serious face. "Let's try, Steve. Let's try not to put each other down. I mean, that's kind of what it's all about, isn't it?"

"They'll never pass a law against it, but it sure is dangerous to your health." He gave her a long kiss on her mouth. "Let's go."

Each of them got into a canoe and paddled off. Halfway across the lake Holly pulled in her paddle and let herself drift. She watched Steve heading for shore, and then she looked back at the island they had left. Her first real boyfriend. She felt that she had crossed an invisible line between childhood and womanhood. An exhilarating thought, with infinite possibilities for the future. Her mother had said that Holly's generation had all the opportunities open to them. They weren't just for what she could *do*, but for what she could *be*. Holly hoped that she would be someone who could love and be loved without giving in exchange her integrity as a woman.

Steve's voice called back to her from near the shore. "Hey, you coming?"

"Yeah. You go along, I'll be in soon."

"You'll be late for supper."

"I don't care, I'm not hungry." The lake was lit up by the rainbow colors of the sunset and Holly could feel the tight strings that had been holding her together loosen. She was aware of a new dimension to her feelings: the intense pleasure of being alone with her thoughts to explore every new emotion, but without the familiar shadow of loneliness. When she got back to camp Steve would be waiting for her. Perhaps that was what being in love meant, to know that someone was there.

About the Author

Hila Colman grew up in New York City and was graduated from Radcliffe College. After college, she did publicity and promotion work; then she wrote articles mor magazines, and, eventually, she began to write books. She has been writing novels for teenagers for many years. "I love teenagers," she says. "I am on their side because they are fluid, fermenting, and rich with life and living."

She lives in Bridgewater, Connecticut, where she is extremely active in the town's government. She is the author of *Sometimes I Don't Love My Mother*, available in a VAGABOND paperback edition from Scholastic Inc.